DATE DUE

OC 8 '02			
JA 1 1 '03			
JY 1 2 '05			
FE 2 3 '06			
DE 2 8 '10			
JY 27 '13			
JY 27 '13			

F
J   Elmer, Robert
         Follow the star

The Young Underground;
Book 7

DEMCO

Books by Robert Elmer

ADVENTURES DOWN UNDER

#1 / *Escape to Murray River*
#2 / *Captive at Kangaroo Springs*
#3 / *Rescue at Boomerang Bend*
#4 / *Dingo Creek Challenge*
#5 / *Race to Wallaby Bay*
#6 / *Firestorm at Kookaburra Station*
#7 / *Koala Beach Outbreak*
#8 / *Panic at Emu Flat*

THE YOUNG UNDERGROUND

#1 / *A Way Through the Sea*
#2 / *Beyond the River*
#3 / *Into the Flames*
#4 / *Far From the Storm*
#5 / *Chasing the Wind*
#6 / *A Light in the Castle*
#7 / *Follow the Star*
#8 / *Touch the Sky*

PROMISE OF ZION

#1 / *Promise Breaker*
#2 / *Peace Rebel*

FOLLOW THE STAR

Robert Elmer

BETHANY HOUSE PUBLISHERS
MINNEAPOLIS, MINNESOTA 55438

Published by Bethany House Publishers
A Ministry of Bethany Fellowship International
11400 Hampshire Avenue South
Minneapolis, Minnesota 55438
www.bethanyhouse.com

Printed in the United States of America by
Bethany Press International, Minneapolis, Minnesota 55438

Library of Congress Cataloging-in-Publication Data

Elmer, Robert.
   Follow the star / Robert Elmer.
     p.   cm. — (The young underground ; #7)
     Summary: In 1945 in Denmark, thirteen-year-old brother and sister
Peter and Elise try to help their Jewish friend Henrik when his mother and
a friend of hers are arrested by the Russians and accused of being spies.
     1. Denmark—History—1900-   —Juvenile fiction. [1. Denmark—
History—1900-   —Fiction. 2. Brothers and sisters—Fiction. 3. Jews—
Denmark—Fiction. 4. Christian life—Fiction.] I. Title. II. Series: Elmer,
Robert. Young underground ; #7.
PZ7.E4794Fo   1996
[Fic]—dc21   96–45836
ISBN 1–55661–660–0   CIP
                                                      AC

To my grandmother (Bedstemor),
Elise Elmer.

ROBERT ELMER has written and edited numerous articles for both newspapers and magazines in the Pacific Northwest. THE YOUNG UNDERGROUND series was inspired by stories from Robert's Denmark-born parents, as well as friends who lived through the years of German occupation. He is currently a writer for an advertising agency in Bellingham, Washington. He and his wife, Ronda, have three children.

CONTENTS

1. Mixed-Up Delivery 9
2. Message From the Past 23
3. The Search 30
4. Race for the Book 43
5. Mysterious Phone Call 50
6. A Cold Welcome 61
7. Unknown Friends 67
8. The First Clue 77
9. Entertaining Angels 91
10. Night Visitor 99
11. Prisoners at the Castle 104
12. Dangerous Voyage 118
13. Race to Danger 137
14. Caroling Party 142
15. Silent Night 146
16. Unexpected Ally 154
17. Follow the Star 169
Epilogue 175

Mixed-Up Delivery
December 7, 1945

"Henrik Melchior!" thundered Mr. Steenstrup. "Do you think you're already on Christmas vacation? For the rest of Denmark, it's still two weeks away."

Henrik snapped his head up from his desk. His dark hair did look a little wild, and there were circles under his brown eyes.

"I'm sorry, Mr. Steenstrup," he gulped.

"Yes, and I'm sure you weren't taking a nap either—no matter how it appeared—but why are you the only one in the class not to turn in your math homework?"

Two rows over, Peter Andersen closed his eyes while his best friend, Henrik, squirmed in his seat. *Not again, Henrik,* thought Peter. *This time Mr. Steenstrup is really blowing a fuse.*

"I was extra busy last night," Henrik started. "I was delivering—I mean, there's no excuse, Mr. Steenstrup."

"I see." Their teacher towered above Henrik in his jet black slacks and freshly pressed white shirt, tapping a heavy wooden ruler in his left hand. Even from his desk, Peter could smell the fresh shaving lotion scent that always followed his teacher in the morning.

All the students in the class seemed to hold their breath, too, waiting for the tall man to deal out the kind of punishment he was feared for. Henrik knit his knuckles in front of him on his little desk and stared straight ahead. Peter could see his friend's bottom lip quivering.

"We'll make it simple this time, Mr. Melchior. You will stay after class until you finish the assignment."

"But, Mr. Steenstrup—" Henrik stopped short when their teacher raised his eyebrows. "Yes, sir."

Peter sighed with the rest of the class. *Maybe Mr. Steenstrup is feeling in the holiday mood already.*

"You'll do it for me, won't you?" Henrik asked Peter and Elise after the class was dismissed for the day. "Just tell Mr. Krogh at the pharmacy that I couldn't make it. I'll lose my job if I don't show up."

"Well . . ." Elise gave her twin brother a worried frown. She looked a lot like Peter—fair skin, slim build, and blond hair. The major difference between the two, besides the obvious fact that she was a girl and Peter was a boy, was that Elise had grown several inches taller than her brother in the past couple of years. Peter had long since given up wondering if or when he would ever catch up, even though kids at school still liked to tease him about it.

"How will we know what to do?" asked Peter.

"Nothing to it," replied Henrik. He was the same age as the twins—thirteen—but was built like an athlete: more muscles, and his knees and elbows didn't stick out. He looked up quickly to see Mr. Steenstrup staring impatiently at him.

"Look," Henrik told them quietly. "Mr. Krogh just gives you a box of things to deliver—stuff like cough syrup and headache pills—and then you drop them off at people's apartments. You know all the streets in town. It's easy."

The tall teacher cleared his throat. "Are you ready, Henrik?"

"Yes, sir," replied Henrik. Then he turned to the twins once more and whispered, "I sure appreciate it. But you'd better get out of here. Mr. Krogh gets mad if I'm even ten seconds late."

Peter and Elise slipped out of the classroom and hurried for the door.

"I suppose this will be just like the old days," Peter said to his sister, "when we used to deliver newspapers for the Underground." He held open the front door.

"Don't remind me, Peter. This isn't the same thing at all. And we need to tell Mom what we're doing first."

"Okay. You run back home, and I'll meet you at the pharmacy."

Peter ran all the way down King Street in the gray half-light of midafternoon. Only three o'clock, and the short winter sunlight was already starting to slip away behind the old buildings of the ancient port city of Helsingor. A bell tinkled when he pushed open the door that read "G. Krogh, Pharmacist."

G. Krogh was bent down behind the counter of his little pharmacy, pulling up blue and green glass bottles and setting them inside a large cardboard box. When he finally looked up, Peter saw an older man with puffs of cotton-ball gray hair clustered around his ears and small, round glasses perched on an enormous triangle of a nose. His rosy cheeks looked as if he had scrubbed them a little too hard.

"Yes?" The man straightened up by pulling on the counter and showed a toothy smile. "Are you with someone?"

Peter didn't like the smell of the pharmacy—it reminded him of the pink calamine lotion his mother put all over him when he was five years old and got a bad sunburn swimming out at the pier on the other side of town. Still, Mr. Krogh didn't look as stern as Henrik had described him.

"Yes," answered Peter. "I mean, no. I'm Peter Andersen. My sister is supposed to be here any minute. Actually, we're Henrik's friends, and we're taking his place for your deliveries this afternoon, if that's all right."

Mr. Krogh wrinkled his brow and put down a green bottle next to the others. "Is he ill?"

"No, he's still at school. He had some work the teacher wanted him to finish. And he knew you wouldn't want him to be late, so we said we would do his deliveries for him."

"We?" Mr. Krogh looked over his glasses again at the door. No one was in sight.

"My sister, Elise, and me."

The pharmacist smiled again and nodded. "All right, then." He scribbled some notes on a few tags and attached them to each bottle with a rubber band. "Here are the deliveries. The list of where they go is inside the box. When you finish, come straight back to the store, and I'll pay you."

Peter nodded once more and looked out the window as Mr. Krogh finished with the tags. *Where's Elise?* Peter wondered.

"You'd better get going, young man," said the pharmacist after a minute. "People are waiting."

"Yes, sir. You can count on us."

Peter took the box in his arms and shuffled out the door, still looking for his sister. Mr. Krogh made a sweeping motion with his hand to hurry him along.

"Okay, where do I go first?" Peter asked himself as he stepped out into the cold afternoon and pulled out the list. He scanned the names for the closest address. "Let's see, one up by the Green Garden train station, a couple on Saint Anne's, then one way over on Esrum Way, and one on Rolf Street, wherever that is. . . ."

His eyes stopped on the last name.

"J. Torp, 44 Saint Anne's Street," he whispered. "Where have I heard that name before?"

He hurried down the street on the way to his first delivery, dodging bicyclists and clutching tightly to his box.

"Peter!" called a familiar voice. "Wait up!"

"There you are," he answered. "I was wondering where you were."

"Mom said to be back by six."

"No problem," answered Peter, turning to meet Elise.

Either Peter wasn't careful enough or the bicyclist was too close, but as Peter turned to talk to his sister, a handlebar caught on the corner of his box, sending it flying into the gutter.

"Oh no!" Peter grabbed for the box but not quickly enough. He looked up to see the bicyclist, but whoever it was had already disappeared, perhaps not even knowing what had happened. Elise rushed over to help him pick up the box.

Peter got down on his knees next to the box, which had somehow landed upright. "All the bottles are probably broken. Mr. Krogh is going to . . . he's going to . . ."

"Maybe not," said Elise, looking inside. Peter was afraid to look.

"Only one is broken," she reported.

"Only one," repeated Peter, peeking inside the box. "But what a mess. There's red cough syrup all over everything."

"It's not that bad," said Elise, carefully picking out the broken bottle with two fingers. "Look, we'll just go back and get another bottle."

"Right, and he's going to give it to us, just like that."

"I'll tell him what happened."

The way it seemed to Peter, he had been attacked by a wild bicyclist and narrowly escaped death. But Elise explained everything the way it really happened, so Mr. Krogh simply shook his head and handed them another bottle.

"It really wasn't his fault," Elise assured him. "It was an accident."

"And you can take the cost of the cough syrup out of what you would have paid us," added Peter for good measure. He looked up at the clock on the back wall of the pharmacy. Maybe if they took long enough, Henrik would catch up with them and save him from this humiliation.

"What makes you think you would earn more than this bottle is worth?" asked the pharmacist.

"Oh," stammered Peter, trying to think of what to say.

"Go." The man waved his hand and gave them a half smile. "Henrik has a couple of good friends to try so hard. Go, before I change my mind and deliver these things myself."

Peter and Elise nodded their thanks and backed out quickly.

A woman walking in the door stepped to the side, and Elise pulled Peter by the arm to get out of her way.

"Thanks, Mr. Krogh," said Elise. "We'll be more careful."

The twins hurried through afternoon crowds on their way to their first delivery.

"New bottle of cough elixir to J. Torp at 44 Saint Anne's Street," said Peter, stepping around a large woman with an armload of brown paper packages.

"Torp," said Elise. "That's the name of that young couple who stayed in Henrik's apartment while the Melchiors were in Sweden during the war."

"That's why it looked familiar," said Peter. "I couldn't remember, since we only met them once. I wonder if they're the same people. Whatever happened to them after Henrik's dad died?"

Elise shrugged and led the way down Saint Anne's, a narrow cobblestone street, barely wider than an alley, in the oldest part of town. Peter knocked on an ancient, weathered door when they arrived at the ground floor apartment a few minutes later. As they waited, his mind wandered back over the past few months since Henrik's father had died of a heart attack. He thought back to the funeral in September. How different Henrik had seemed ever since—as if he were still mad at someone for what happened. Other times, he was just kind of far off. Different. Not like the joke-telling, always-smiling Henrik. Peter didn't blame Henrik, but sometimes it was hard to know what to do or how to act around him.

Elise took a turn knocking, and then they heard a shuffling sound from inside.

"Yes?" said an old woman peeking out from behind her door. Her face looked as old as the door. Definitely not one of the young people who had stayed in Henrik's apartment.

"Krogh Pharmacy delivery," announced Peter, holding out a bottle.

"What happened to the other young man?" she asked, pulling a knitted white shawl closer around her shoulders.

Elise tried to smile. "We're just filling in for Henrik."

"I see. Then you've brought my headache pills?"

Peter looked down at the bottle in confusion. "Uh, no, this looks like cough elixir. Oh, and it says it's for Mr. Norbjerg."

The old woman crossed her arms and gave them both an annoyed look. "Do I look like a Mr. Norbjerg? Why would I want cough elixir when I don't have a cough? Can you tell me that?"

Peter quickly searched through the box. "Headache pills, headache pills . . . here they are. I must have gotten my list mixed up. I'm sorry, Mrs. Nor—I mean, Mrs. Torp." He gave her a bottle of pills with the right name on it.

She held the bottle to her face and studied it for a moment. "This would never have happened with the other young man," she muttered. "He knew the difference between cough elixir and headache pills. And there's something sticky all over this bottle."

"Yes, ma'am." By that time, Peter wanted to leave her with the entire jumbled box and just go home. "I'm sorry about the mix-up."

"Mr. Krogh is going to hear about this," she grumbled.

"Um, one more thing," said Peter as the woman started to close her door. "Are you related to a younger couple named Torp that used to live in a Jewish family's apartment during the war? Over on Star Street?"

The woman looked at them strangely, as if she didn't quite understand what Peter had asked her. Then her face lit up.

"You know my nephew Ole?" she asked.

"Yes, I mean no. They stayed in Henrik's apartment because—"

"Henrik? Who's Henrik?"

Elise stepped up. "Henrik is your regular delivery boy. He—"

"Yes, yes. Well, what do you know," she interrupted. "I didn't realize my delivery boy was a friend of Ole. Of course, Ole and his wife moved away, you know. Ole got a real nice new job, and Gerta is going to go back to school. I think she wanted to be a nurse. Only thing is, I don't know yet what town they moved to. I did tell them, though, before they left, that they should settle down and have some children. . . ."

Peter backed away from the door as old Mrs. Torp kept up her speech about her nephew. He nodded as she spoke.

"Yes, ma'am. Well, we'd better get going."

"Oh yes." She seemed to catch herself, then smiled for the first time. Maybe she had forgotten about calling Mr. Krogh to complain about the mix-up. "I'm glad to have met one of my nephew's friends. Have a very good Christmas."

"Merry Christmas," Peter and Elise sang back.

They retreated back down Saint Anne's Street to the next address while Elise tried to sort out the rest of the bottles.

"I have a feeling this is going to be a long afternoon," Peter said quietly.

———————

"Hey, Henrik!" yelled Peter as he and Elise came around the street corner in front of Henrik's apartment on Star Street. "What are you staring at?"

Henrik had stopped in the middle of the sidewalk and was looking up, arms crossed. Even though it was only five o'clock, it was already dark as night. Only a dim light glowed from the Melchiors' window.

"I don't think he heard you," Elise told her brother as they stepped over the leash of a little collie who was dragging her master in front of the twins.

"Hey, Henrik!" Peter tried once more. This time his friend jumped and looked quickly around to see who had called. By that time, the twins were standing next to him.

"Oh, hi, you guys." Henrik scanned the street quickly, as if checking to see who else had seen him. His dark eyebrows were knitted with worry, his forehead wrinkled in a frown. "So how did it go? Did you just finish?"

Peter blew out his cheeks and made a puff of steam in the chilly night air. "Ten deliveries."

"Oh." Henrik paused for a second to think. "That shouldn't have taken very long. I hope you didn't get lost."

"Not lost," explained Elise.

"Just a little mixed-up," added Peter with a smile.

"Oh." Henrik seemed miles away. "Well, I sure appreciate you two covering for me."

"No problem," answered Peter, looking up to see what Henrik was staring at. Henrik didn't make any move to go inside, and Peter wondered why they were standing out in the cold. Peter glanced at a Christmas dress display in a fabric shop window, then shivered despite his wool coat, fuzzy black earmuffs, and thick, knitted scarf. The sign inside the display read "Only Three Weeks Until Christmas," but the message didn't excite him the way it usually did. He shoved his hands into his coat pockets to keep them warm.

"We've hardly seen you in the past few weeks, Henrik," he finally said, tracing a pattern with his toe in the slush of the sidewalk.

"Ever since you got your job," put in Elise.

Henrik looked down at his feet, then back up to the window. An icy sleet began to fall, and the dull yellow light in the window above them seemed to grow brighter in the gloom.

"Yeah, well, since my father's not here anymore, somebody has to make a little extra money."

Instantly Peter regretted opening his mouth. He started to turn.

"Wait a minute," said Henrik. "Why don't we go inside for a minute?"

A light from the pawnshop next door fell on the narrow black door, shining weakly on the brass plate with Henrik's father's name: E. Melchior.

"It *is* kind of cold," admitted Elise.

Peter and Elise stomped up the stairs, kicking slush from their feet. Henrik put his finger to his lips to shush the twins, then slowly opened the door. Peter and Elise looked at each other in surprise, wondering why Henrik was being so secretive, but they played along, tiptoeing quietly to the hall closet to hang up their coats.

"It's okay now," Henrik finally said in a whisper. "I've been back home once already this afternoon since Mr. Steenstrup let me out, and they didn't even notice."

They? Peter wondered who Henrik was talking about. Was someone else staying with Henrik and his mom?

"Hey, you know," began Elise, "maybe we could all study a couple of things for the math test next week. . . ." Elise's voice trailed off.

All three of them stood still when they heard a man's voice from inside the Melchiors' living room. Then, for the first time since before the funeral, they heard Mrs. Melchior's cheery laugh.

"You liked that joke, did you?" came the deep voice. None of the kids could move. They just stood listening in the entryway.

"Well, how about the one where someone asked the *schlemiel*, 'Why do you people always answer a question with another question?' And then the schlemiel answers, 'Why shouldn't we?' "

There was more laughter, but Henrik didn't smile. Instead he wadded up his wet coat, threw it to the floor next to his boots, and stalked past the living room. Peter and Elise tiptoed behind him, staying in the hallway.

"What's a 'schlem—,' or whatever that word was, Henrik?" asked Peter.

Henrik answered without turning around. "Schlemiel." He pronounced the Jewish word carefully for them, like shluh-MEAL. "A dimwit. Jewish jokes are full of schlemiels. And speaking of—"

"Well, look who's finally back from his hard work!" boomed the cheery man's voice from the living room. Peter looked into the room to see a trim-looking man with dark hair and a short-cropped dark beard sitting in a comfortable chair in the corner. Mrs. Melchior sat by herself on the couch. The man's dark eyes blinked behind the thick bottle-cap lenses of his glasses in a way that instantly made Peter smile. He and Elise stopped, but Henrik tried to keep walking down the hallway.

"Henrik, we were worried about you," said Mrs. Melchior, getting to her feet.

"We?" whispered Henrik under his breath. No one else heard the comment except Peter. Still in the hallway, Henrik stopped without turning around and leaned against the wallpaper.

"Come in here for a minute, Henrik," continued Henrik's mother. "I know you have a lot of work to do with your job. But if you're going to be late on these dark nights, you need to tell me what you're doing."

Henrik nodded. "Sorry, Mother. Actually, Peter and Elise did the deliveries for me tonight. I had to stay and do some math after school. And then I walked around a little."

"Oh," replied Mrs. Melchior. She was a petite woman, dark-haired like her son, with a trace of the same athletic build and the same sharp features. Peter was surprised to see her wearing one of her nicer dresses, maroon with a lace collar.

"That was very nice of them," she continued, "only I hope you're not getting into trouble at school. Are you, Henrik?"

"I'm fine, Mother."

Henrik's mother didn't look convinced. "Well, you wash up for dinner. You remember Mr. Karlsson from Sweden, don't you?"

"I remember," mumbled Henrik, still not turning around.

Peter was starting to get nervous at the way Henrik was acting.

Mrs. Melchior waved her hand at the twins, and they stepped in from the hallway. "And these are Henrik's friends, Peter and Elise."

Elise and Peter both shook hands politely when the stranger stood to greet them, and Peter couldn't help smiling back at the man's honest grin.

"I'm Matthias," the man told them as he gripped their hands. "I knew Henrik's father from some business dealings, then when the Melchiors were in Hälsinborg in Sweden during the war, I . . . ah . . ."

"You helped more than you know," added Mrs. Melchior, looking at the back of Henrik's head. "Henrik, please come say hello to Mr. Karlsson—I mean, Matthias."

Everyone watched Henrik as he slowly came in from the hallway, then marched over with his head down to shake the man's outstretched hand.

"Happy Hanukkah, Henrik," said Matthias with the same infectious smile as before. Mrs. Melchior sank back in the couch with a sigh, looking sadly at her son.

"Your mother asked me to come help light your Hanukkah candles with you," said the man named Matthias, pumping Henrik's limp hand and waiting in vain for the boy to look up. "And since it's the eighth day, we're going to light all eight candles, right?"

Henrik bent over to unlace his shoes and again mumbled under his breath. "That's not *your* job," Peter thought he heard him say.

When Henrik straightened up, Matthias held out a small box of matches to him. "I thought you'd want to do the honors, since you're the man of the house now."

Henrik looked surprised but took the matches. He walked over to the traditional brass Jewish candleholder on the kitchen windowsill. Eight tall white candles were arranged in a row, each one in its own stem, leading down to a single stand. It looked a little like a brass tree with eight even branches.

When everyone had gathered around the candles, Matthias began reciting something in a foreign language. Peter didn't understand a word, but he was sure it was Hebrew. He remembered Henrik telling him a few Hebrew words that his father had taught him, and this sounded a lot like that. Matthias was holding a small book open close to his face. Peter caught a glimpse of the strange-looking letters on the page, and he wondered how anyone could read them.

Then the man nodded. "Go ahead, Henrik."

Henrik took out a match and scratched it on the side of the matchbox three times before it came to life. He paused as the match sputtered, then flared up. He lit one candle after another until all eight were blazing brightly.

Elise caught her breath. "That's pretty."

"The final night of Hanukkah," continued Matthias with a smile. "We celebrate the miracle of God, when the Jewish people returned to the temple and one day's worth of oil in the lamp kept burning for eight. We celebrate God's victory."

For a moment, Peter felt like someone at a birthday party without an invitation. In all the years they had known Henrik, Peter and Elise had never seen this candle-lighting ceremony. The only other time Peter had witnessed a Jewish holiday with Henrik's family was over two years back when he had been invited to share in their Rosh Hashana dinner. But that had been a long time ago, when Henrik's father was still alive.

"Many candles can be kindled from one candle without making it less bright," recited Matthias, closing his eyes and rocking slightly on his heels. The apartment was completely dark, except for the eight candles. Completely quiet, except for the quiet voice of Matthias. "That's from the Mishna."

Peter didn't dare ask what Matthias had meant, but Mrs. Melchior leaned over and put her hands on his and Elise's shoulders. "The Mishna is a collection of Jewish sayings from some of the famous old rabbis," she whispered in their ears. They both nodded.

Henrik stood facing the candles, his hands on his hips. "Done?" he asked, almost crossly.

Mrs. Melchior reached for the kitchen light switch and frowned. Peter blinked as his eyes got used to the bright electric lamp again.

"No, not quite," she replied. "I thought you might like to exchange a couple of Hanukkah presents. Or maybe you're too old for that now."

"Presents?" Henrik looked surprised. "I thought—"

"What did you think?" asked his mother as she pulled out a small bundle from a kitchen cabinet and handed it to him. "You think we're going to stop celebrating Hanukkah now simply because your father isn't . . ."

Her voice trembled, but Matthias spoke up. "I hope you don't mind that I brought a couple of presents as well." He disappeared for a moment into the next room, returning with a large, bulging brown paper sack.

"I'm sorry we don't have presents for all our guests," he continued. "But I suppose they'll get their turn at Christmas. Pretty soon." He winked at Peter.

"So open it, Henrik," said Elise. "You always open your presents as if they're some kind of bomb."

Henrik looked uncertainly at his mother, then slipped off the twine, pulled off the paper, and held up a warm-looking blue wool long-sleeve shirt.

"You needed another warm one," explained his mother.

Henrik finally smiled. "Thanks."

Matthias looked from Henrik to Mrs. Melchior. He reached into his sack, pulled out a box of what looked like hand soap, and gave it to Henrik's mother.

"It's really nothing," he stammered. "But I hear it's still hard to find over here in Denmark. We have it in Sweden, though."

"Oh, thank you, Matthias," bubbled Mrs. Melchior. She held the soap to her face and smelled it. "Even after seven months, they're still rationing a few things. And it smells so nice."

Henrik was trying on his shirt, but he lost his smile once more when Matthias pulled out another bundle from his bag and held it out toward him.

"This isn't a present from me, Henrik. It's from your father."

MESSAGE FROM THE PAST

Henrik stopped buttoning his shirt and looked hard at Matthias. "What do you mean? Where did you get it?"

"I was at the hospital where your father . . . died," Matthias began. "Somehow a few of your father's things were moved around. This was in a lost-and-found box, and I told them I would bring it to you."

Henrik took what looked like a small braided rug from Matthias, white-and-black with tassels along one edge. An envelope fell out when he unfolded it.

"Oh, and I forgot to tell you. There's a letter to you in there, too. They found it with the shawl."

"What is it?" whispered Peter.

Mrs. Melchior looked away and back at the Hanukkah candles still burning brightly in the window. "It was Mr. Melchior's prayer shawl, the one that belonged to Henrik's great-grandfather. We couldn't find it during the last days at the hospital."

Peter still wasn't sure how a prayer shawl worked or even what it was for, but he could tell it had to be something special by the way Henrik handled it.

"Read the note, son," urged Mrs. Melchior.

Henrik clutched the letter and looked up at Matthias. "Later, I think. When there aren't so many people around."

Matthias took a deep breath and put his hands together in a silent clap. "Yes, well, it's time for me to go, Ruth. It's getting late."

Mrs. Melchior's voice went hoarse, and she gave her son a mortified look, as if he had just burped at the table or dropped a potato on the floor. "I'm terribly sorry, Matthias. You don't have to go so soon, do you? Couldn't you stay for dinner?"

But Matthias shook his head and went to the coat closet. "Thank you for the invitation. But I . . . I must be going." He quickly bundled himself up and shook both Peter's and Elise's hands once more.

"Hope to see you two again," he said with a smile. "Perhaps we'll have more of a chance to talk next time." He looked over at Henrik, who was trying to get away from the strong grip of his mother's hand on his shoulder.

"Thanks for, uh, bringing my father's stuff over," Henrik finally mumbled, then ducked away.

"I'm glad I could do it." Matthias smiled as if he and Henrik were the best of friends.

But Matthias was barely out the door when Mrs. Melchior exploded. "Henrik Melchior, I have never been so embarrassed in my life!"

Peter and Elise looked at each other, and they both found their coats as quickly as Matthias had found his. "Um, we better get going, too," said Peter.

"Well, what was he doing here, anyway?" answered Henrik, suddenly very busy with setting two plates and glasses on the kitchen table. "He didn't have any business coming over."

"Yes, he did, Henrik." His mother's dark eyes flashed with anger. "He's a pilot. He flew his small plane over just to give you your father's prayer shawl."

"Yeah, and maybe he'll take you for a ride sometime."

"He was your father's friend, and there has been nothing improper about him helping us to straighten out some of our finances. He is *not* a boyfriend!"

"Well? He was pretending like he was my father. I don't like him."

"That was pretty obvious," said his mother, turning away. She put her hand to her face and wiped her eye with a napkin.

"See you later, Henrik," said Peter, opening the door.

"Wait," he told them suddenly. "I'll go with you down the block. I'll be right back, Mother."

Henrik's mother said nothing as she retreated to a back room.

"Wow, Henrik," said Peter when they were outside on the dark street. "That was pretty tense. Why did you do that?"

"Don't you think you could have been a little more polite to that guy?" asked Elise. "He was just trying to be nice."

"It's not right," spat Henrik. "It's been what—only three months since my dad died? That guy's just a schlemiel. Makes me sick."

"Oh, come on," argued Elise. "He brought those things back for you. What's wrong with that?"

"I don't like the way he did all that Hanukkah stuff in Hebrew. Then he starts quoting from the Mishna and everything. What a show-off."

Peter looked over his shoulder to see the Hanukkah candles in the Melchior window still burning. "I don't know, Henrik. I thought it was neat, until you started attacking him. . . ."

"You two both sound like you're on his side."

"There aren't any sides, Henrik," answered Elise. "It was just kind of embarrassing, the way you acted."

They walked on in silence for a couple more blocks. Peter pulled up his collar against the falling sleet; the tiny chunks of ice seemed to dribble from the sky like salt out of a saltshaker. The ice drifted sideways across the yellow glow of a streetlight, then down the sidewalk, where it melted into a dirty silver-gray porridge.

Finally Henrik cleared his throat. "I still don't think he should have come."

"At least he brought you your great-grandfather's prayer shawl and that letter," whispered Elise.

"The letter," said Henrik, stopping in his tracks. "That's right."

Henrik pulled his father's letter out of his pocket and held it up in the light from a bakery they were walking past. They could barely make out the lettering, but Henrik slipped open the envelope flap with his thumb.

He leaned close to the bakery window to catch more light from inside. The shop was closed, but Peter could see a man in the back room mixing something in a large metal bowl. He looked up curiously, wiped his hands on his apron, then resumed his work.

" 'Dear son,' " began Henrik, almost in a whisper.

"Henrik," interrupted Elise. "You didn't want to read that note with people around, and now you're going to read it in the middle of the street?"

"I wasn't talking about you. I just want to see what it says. Stay here for a minute, would you?"

Something in Henrik's voice kept them from moving. He lowered his voice again to continue reading. " 'Hope you're doing well at the Andersens. I miss . . .' "

Henrik's voice quivered, and he lowered the letter. There weren't many people on the dark street, but in the distance they could hear the bells of Saint Olai Church. Peter counted six rings. Their mother would be worried about them. Henrik closed his eyes and held out the letter to Elise.

"Uh . . . there's not enough light here. Read this for me?"

"But, Henrik," she hesitated, not taking the letter from his hand. "It sounds pretty personal. I'd better not . . ."

"Please? It's just a regular letter, like he always wrote me. I can't read it right now. But I have to know what it says."

Suddenly a pile of slush from the bakery roof slid down on top of them, landing squarely on the letter and knocking it out of Henrik's hands.

"Oh no!" he cried, looking down at the sidewalk.

Peter got down on his knees and quickly retrieved the soggy

paper, then tried to shake off the water.

"It's ruined!" wailed Henrik. "The ink is running all over."

"No, it's not," answered Elise, taking the letter. "Not everywhere."

She leaned down into the light from the bakery window as Henrik had done, and Peter looked over her shoulder to see if he could make out anything. But as Henrik had feared, at least half the writing had turned into a blurry sea of black ink.

"Start over again," suggested Peter. "Maybe we can figure it out." Elise nodded and began to read.

" 'Dear son,' " she began, clearing her throat. " 'Hope you're doing well at the Andersens. I miss . . .' "

She paused, turning the paper over in her hands. "It goes on for a couple of sentences, but then I think it says something about 'feeling better.' This next line is wiped out. Okay, here's something I can read: 'I haven't even mentioned this to your mother yet, but it's something I've been thinking about for a long time. I have something very important to discuss with you. . . .' "

By that time, the baker had come out to the front part of his shop and was looking at them curiously. Peter waved, and the man smiled.

"Then there's something about Jerusalem, I think," she continued.

"Jerusalem?" asked Peter. "What are you talking about?"

Elise shook her head and pointed to a faded word. "Doesn't make any sense. But that's what it looks like. Then there's something about a book," she continued. "No, a letter. 'So we can talk about this, I want you to bring me a few letters. They're inside a book. A Hebrew book . . .' "

"Is that all?" Henrik hovered over Elise.

"A little more," answered Elise, shaking the paper again. "It says, 'You'll find the book back home in our apartment, on top of the kitchen cabinet next to the stove. Bring it back to me with the letters next time you come to visit me at the hospital, and . . .' "

Elise lowered the letter and looked at the two boys. "That's all

I can read. Except for at the bottom where it looks like he signed it. I'm sorry, Henrik."

"That's okay. Thanks," said Henrik, taking the letter back and smoothing it out against the leg of his pants.

"Sounds like it was pretty important," said Peter.

Henrik just shook his head and folded the ruined letter. "So why didn't he tell me about it before?"

"I don't know," answered Peter as he and Elise hurried away. "But we'd better get home before we get into trouble. You better, too."

"I'll call you," Henrik yelled back as he disappeared into the shadows of Star Street.

———

An hour later, while Peter and Elise were trying to catch up on their homework, Henrik called.

"I looked exactly where my dad said it would be," Henrik insisted over the phone. "It wasn't there. Nothing was there."

"Are you sure?" asked Peter. He stood in the Andersen kitchen, twirling the telephone cord around his finger.

"Ask him if he checked down behind the stove," whispered Elise, who was leaning close to the receiver to listen in. "Maybe it fell."

"I heard that," answered Henrik. "Tell Elise I looked there. I looked everywhere. My mom says she remembers Father used to keep a Hebrew book there, but it's gone now."

"What do you mean, it's gone?" asked Peter.

"I mean, remember the people who lived here while we were in Sweden?"

"You mean the Torps? Henrik, they were really nice. They wouldn't have stolen anything."

"I didn't say that, Peter. I know they took good care of our apartment. It's just that, well, we never even met them. Maybe they put the book in a box somewhere when they were cleaning."

"What about the Jerusalem thing?" asked Peter. "Did you ask your mom if she knew what that meant?"

Henrik didn't answer.

"Henrik?"

"I'm here. Uh, I think my dad maybe wanted to visit the Holy Land or something."

Peter wasn't sure why his friend suddenly seemed so nervous.

"So what are you going to do, Henrik?"

"I'm going to find out what happened to the Torps, and then I'm going to find out where my father's book with the letters is— if it's the last thing I do."

THE SEARCH

"Okay, it's been two weeks now, Elise," Peter told his sister as they ran out the door on their way to Henrik's apartment. "Let's not say anything else to Henrik about that book."

"Don't worry. I learned my lesson last time we asked." Elise held her hand out to see if it was still raining, then wiped the sprinkle on the front of Peter's shirt inside his unbuttoned raincoat. "It's just that he's been so depressed since the day we read the note from his dad. And then when he couldn't find that book. . . ."

Peter glanced up as they walked. "Yeah, I know. Too bad he can't look forward to Christmas. So did you get me a pencil set again?"

"Peter Andersen! How do you know I got you *anything*?"

Peter smiled. "Just a hunch. I figure since you've given me a pencil set for the past three years, maybe . . ."

"Maybe this year will be different," finished Elise.

"I'll tell you what I got for you," he offered.

"No deal. Besides, I already know."

"You do not!" Peter tried to remember where he had hidden

the hairbrush he had bought for Elise a week ago. Maybe she *had* found it. . . .

Elise simply smiled her "I know the answer" kind of smile and kept walking. Up ahead, on the other side of the street, someone was running their way.

"Is that Henrik?" Peter wondered aloud.

"Happy Saturday morning!" yelled Henrik a moment later. Even from a distance, Peter could tell he was wearing a wide smile. A car honked as their friend darted across to meet them, but Henrik didn't pay attention.

"Hey, you two!" Henrik splashed in a puddle with both feet, trying to get them wet. He wasn't even wearing a raincoat. "I couldn't wait for you to come my way, so I thought I'd meet you. Guess what?"

"I'm afraid to ask," said Elise.

Henrik skipped backward in front of the twins. "I finally found out something about those people who were taking care of our apartment. Gerta and Ole Torp."

"How?" asked Peter.

Henrik sighed, and his cheery smile changed to a frown. "That's the only bad part. Matthias asked around. Said he wanted to help me. I think he's trying to be some kind of buddy so I'll like him."

"No kidding," said Peter.

"What's wrong with that?" asked Elise.

Henrik didn't answer, and his smile returned. "Anyway, I found out the Torps moved just out of town, to Hillerod."

Peter scratched his hair underneath the hood of his raincoat. "But you don't know their address? That reminds me. We ran into an old lady a couple of weeks ago . . . did I tell you? This woman was related to them, but all she could tell us was that they had moved. She had ordered some headache pills."

"Huh?" Henrik gave them a funny look. "What do headache pills have to do with it?"

"Well, it turned out to be a major headache," answered Peter.

"We almost gave her the wrong medicine the day we ran your errands."

"You never told me about that."

Peter wished he hadn't gone into the details.

"But there can't be too many Torps around," added Elise, avoiding a puddle. "It's not a common name like Andersen or Nielsen or Petersen. We should be able to find out where they live."

"That's what I mean," chirped Henrik as they reached his home. "And now I have a plan to find out just where—only don't tell Matthias if we see him again. He's been flying his little plane over from Sweden way too often lately—*says* he has business in Copenhagen."

"Don't tell him what?" Peter wanted to know.

"Don't tell him that we're finally going to get to the bottom of this missing book mystery this weekend. We're going to find out what those letters are all about, and we're going to find out why it was so important for me to bring them to my dad."

Peter and Elise stopped for a minute in the drizzle as Henrik jogged up the stairs to his apartment. He paused, turned around, and waved for them to follow.

"If he has a plan . . ." began Elise.

"Then we're in for trouble," finished Peter. "I know, that's what worries me, too."

Inside his room, Henrik flopped down on his bed. "Okay, so here's what we're going to do to find these people. Hillerod is only half an hour away by bus."

Peter still didn't understand. "But we still don't have their address, right? And Hillerod isn't a small town."

"Details. All we have to do is get there and ask around."

"You really think our parents would let us?" wondered Peter.

"I've already asked my mother," replied Henrik.

Elise stood up. "And she said?"

Almost as an answer, the twins and Henrik heard Mrs. Melchior call from the kitchen.

"Peter and Elise, we're having lunch in a few minutes. Can you stay, too?"

Henrik launched himself off the bed and looked down the hallway. "What does she mean, 'too'?"

The twins followed Henrik into the kitchen, and when Henrik stopped short, they ran into him like a train wreck.

"Hi, kids," boomed Matthias Karlsson. Peter peeked around Henrik to see the family friend sitting at the kitchen table. "You're all staying for lunch? It's already after noon."

"Oh," whispered Henrik in a disappointed tone. "Didn't hear you come in."

"Thank you, Mrs. Melchior," said Elise. "I'll call my mom."

Before Henrik could embarrass himself further, Matthias popped up from his chair with a smile and headed for the door. "Let me get those other things for you, Ruth. They're out in the car. I'll be right back."

When the door slammed behind Matthias, Mrs. Melchior looked at her son and raised her hands. "Before you say anything, Henrik, I want you to get this straight about Matthias."

"But what is the deal with him calling you 'Ruth,' like—"

"That's enough, Henrik," she interrupted. "You don't seem to understand that Matthias is just a former friend of your father's who is helping—"

"But, Mother—"

"No, let me finish."

Henrik fidgeted while Mrs. Melchior continued talking. Matthias would be back from the car any moment.

"It's been hard for all of us since your father died, but Matthias has been kind to us. He's helped with a lot of the legal paper work, a lot of the money things. I've tried to explain that to you before. You're not making it easier for me with this terrible attitude of yours."

"I don't have a terrible attitude."

"Well, I sure don't know what else to call it. After the way you treated Matthias when he was here two weeks ago, I'm surprised he came back at all. I'm not going to let you do that again."

Henrik's mouth hung slack.

"So I'm going to make you a deal. I'll let you take the bus to Hillerod on three conditions. One, if Peter and Elise's parents say it's okay for them to go with you."

Henrik lit up. "No problem, Mother."

"We haven't asked them yet," interrupted Peter, but no one seemed to hear him.

"Two, if you're home by dinnertime. That will give you the rest of the afternoon."

Again Henrik smiled. "We'll be home with the book way before that. But what's the third thing?"

"The third thing is if you promise to change your attitude about Matthias and not make another scene."

Henrik bit his lip. "I don't know. . . ."

Mrs. Melchior held out her hand for her son to shake. "All three or nothing. Deal?"

Henrik took a deep breath. Finally he put out his hand—but slowly. "Deal, but don't tell him."

––––––––

"You really think we'll be home by dinner?" asked Elise, looking out the bus window at the rain. The steady drizzle hadn't let up all day, coating every building with a wet reminder of the Danish winter. Peter sat beside her, holding on to the back of the seat in front of him where Henrik sat.

"Absolutely," said Henrik. "But we're already late, thanks to your cat." He crossed his arms with a satisfied look and leaned his head over backward to stare at the twins.

"Tiger can't help it." Peter smiled and looked back out the window of the bus. "He likes to follow us."

"Yeah, but what would we have done if he'd followed us all the way onto the bus instead of just down the street?"

Peter shrugged. "I don't know. He could have come with us maybe?"

Henrik finally smiled and shook his head. "You have one strange cat, Peter, the way he follows you around."

"So what exactly is your plan, Henrik?" Elise changed the subject.

"All we do is stop in at the post office and ask where the Torps live. The post office will know, if anyone does. Then we go to the Torps' house and get the book, and you can get back home and get ready for Christmas like your mom wanted."

Elise put her hand to her forehead.

"What's wrong, Elise?" asked Peter.

"Was that really your plan?" she asked.

"Sure," answered Henrik. "What do you mean?"

"It's Saturday, Henrik," she continued. "Saturday. Post offices close early on Saturday."

Henrik pulled his head back straight and didn't say anything for a moment. "I guess I forgot about that," he whispered. "What time do they close?"

"Two o'clock," answered Elise.

Peter looked at his wristwatch. "That gives us about five minutes to get there."

Outside they could see the tall, pointed towers of the impressive U-shaped Frederiksborg Castle, set out into the city's castle lake. During the summer, thousands of tourists flocked to Hillerod, the city that grew up around the royal castle. But not on a rainy December afternoon.

"Maybe if we run . . ." Peter began, but Henrik wasn't listening. A minute later, the bus jolted to a halt, and the bus driver looked up into his rearview mirror to see who was getting out at the city's first stop.

"Where's the post office?" asked Henrik, poised like a runner at a track meet.

"Two blocks down there." The driver pointed with a jab of his chin down a side street, and Henrik shot out the door. Their friend had disappeared into the drizzle before Peter and Elise had even stood up.

Elise shook her head as they stepped away from the bus. "I don't know if he's going to make it in time," she told Peter.

Peter checked his watch again as they made their way down

a slippery sidewalk in the same direction Henrik had run. Five after two. A minute later, they were standing in front of a trim, brick two-story building with Henrik, staring into the dark lobby of the city's main post office.

"I thought for sure somebody would be here a couple of minutes late," said Henrik, his voice cracking. He pounded on the glass front door.

Elise shook her head. "That's okay. Maybe we can think of another way to find these Torp people."

Henrik looked down at the wet sidewalk. "Yeah, but how? I should have thought it out better. It's my fault."

"Forget it, Henrik," ventured Peter. "I have an idea."

Henrik brightened up. "You do?"

"Sure. See those buildings down that way?" Peter pointed down the street at some taller apartment complexes that lined the main road, with typical Danish brick sides and bright red tile roofs. "We just split up and start knocking on doors. When someone answers, we ask, 'Do you have Henrik's book?' until we find the right people."

Elise laughed, but Henrik frowned.

"Just kidding, Henrik," added Peter.

Henrik stared up at the rain, which had turned into a steady downpour. "You two are the only ones who know what the Torps look like."

"Oh," stammered Peter. "Well, we only saw them a couple of times when you were in Sweden. I'm not sure they would remember us, anyway."

"So what did they look like?" murmured Henrik over the noise of the rain pelting the streets. The twins started out after him again as he marched down the rainy sidewalk, past restaurants and stores. Everyone else on the street had black umbrellas like Elise, but that didn't stop the wind from blowing the cold December rain in sideways and soaking them from the knees down. Henrik ignored the rain, marching along ahead in his dark raincoat. His black hair was soon pasted to his head.

"He was kind of big-boned," replied Elise, balancing the umbrella like a shield against the wind. "Henrik, there's enough room for you under the umbrella."

Henrik just waved and half smiled back at her. "I'm okay, thanks. Big-boned . . . you mean chubby?"

Peter shook his head. "No, he was like Elise said. Kind of big and wide. Looked like a farmer, but I think he's an accountant or something."

"Okay." Henrik kept walking as if he knew where he was going. "What else? What about her? I want to make sure I would recognize these people if we met them on the street."

"She was almost as big as he was," continued Elise. "I remember her hands—they were real strong looking."

"Great," said Henrik, quickening his pace and stepping through a puddle on the sidewalk. "So all I have to do is look for a man with big bones and a woman with strong hands, and that will be them for sure."

Peter looked at his sister, still struggling with the umbrella. "Well, I think I'd recognize them, wouldn't you? Where are we going, anyway?"

"I think Henrik took your joke about knocking on doors seriously," she told him just before a gust of wind grabbed the umbrella and turned it completely inside out.

"Hold on to it!" cried Peter. For a moment, it looked as if Elise would take off, but she quickly pulled the wild umbrella back in.

"Oh dear." She managed only to straighten it halfway back into shape, but one of the metal ribs had ripped through the fabric. Peter had to laugh as he tried to help her reclaim their only shelter from the storm.

"Looks pretty dead," he said finally, giving up on the umbrella. He was mostly dry under his yellow slicker, but water was starting to drip down the back of his neck.

Henrik was waiting for them at the end of the block, where the street changed from small shops to larger apartment buildings.

"You two ready?" he called to them. "I'll take this row of buildings if you take the other."

"I was kidding about knocking on doors," offered Peter, but Henrik looked too determined.

"We're not going to knock on doors," replied Henrik. "All we have to do is go inside the main entrance of each building and check the names on the mailboxes."

Peter looked down the street, counted ten buildings on each side, and took a deep breath. "Okay, here we go."

"We can leapfrog buildings," Elise told him as they reached the first building. "You go to one, then I'll go to the next one."

Peter nodded.

After the first couple of buildings, it became routine. Push open the door to the lobby, find the wall full of mail slots, look at each one for names, then run out to the next building.

"Slowpoke!" Elise yelled to him as she skipped to the building in front.

"Wait up," Peter yelled back. "My buildings are bigger."

Henrik was doing the same thing on the other side of the street, only not quite as fast. Building after building, around the corner, to the rail yards on one side and the castle lake on the other. An hour passed, then two, and still there seemed to be no end to the row of buildings.

Finally Peter stopped to catch his breath. He waved at Elise when she came out of a smaller building on a corner.

"Wait a minute, Elise," he huffed. "Let's wait for Henrik."

Elise looked up at the sky, nodded, and crossed her arms. As they stood on the corner under an awning, Peter wiggled his toes and listened to the squishing sound of his wet socks inside his wet shoes. It started to rain even harder.

"There you are," shouted Henrik as he slogged across the street. Soaked to the bone, he swiped the water from his forehead and stopped in front of them. "No luck?"

Elise shivered. "It's getting really dark, Henrik."

They stood on the street corner for a minute and listened to the rain pelting the awning. Then Elise pulled something out of her pocket and held it out to the boys.

"Hey, black licorice." Henrik smiled and took a piece. "Our

favorite food. Where did you get it?"

Elise nibbled the tail of her miniature licorice cat. "Grandfather gave it to me the other day. He said to share."

Peter chewed on his piece thoughtfully and looked up at the dark sky. "If we don't catch the four-thirty bus, Henrik, we're in trouble. I think it's the last one."

"That still gives us a couple of minutes," replied Henrik. "I hate to give up when we're so close."

"Maybe," said Peter, still chewing. "But there's no way to find these people unless we come back on a weekday."

Henrik crossed his arms and grumbled to himself.

"We've got to get out of this rain for a minute, Henrik," insisted Elise. Henrik opened his mouth as if to object, then nodded weakly and followed Elise as she turned to enter a small shop.

As Peter opened the door, he was hit hard by the mouthwatering fragrance of a delicatessen.

"My stomach realizes it's almost time for dinner," said Peter, taking a deep breath. He closed his eyes and imagined a thickly buttered slice of black rye bread piled high with cheese and salami.

Several shoppers were standing in front of the glass counter, picking out sausages and cheeses. Some already had arms full of packages, and most chattered happily, as if they were in a holiday mood. A little girl out with her mother stared at them. Elise folded her umbrella carefully and straightened her hair.

"Nice and warm in here," she told Peter quietly.

Peter enjoyed the warmth of the store, too, as he watched the water from his raincoat make little puddles on the floor. Next to him, Henrik fidgeted.

"Can I help you kids?" asked a white-aproned man from behind the counter as the shoppers ahead of them turned to go. The bells on the door jingled cheerily as they left the shop. Peter checked his pockets, but he knew he had exactly enough change for his bus ticket home and nothing more.

"Uh, just getting out of the rain," explained Peter. The delicatessen door jingled once more.

"Hey, Nils" came a man's voice in back of them. "Who ordered all the rain? I'm trying to finish my deliveries today, and it's making me late."

The big man in the white apron smiled. "Sorry about that. Any mail for me this afternoon?"

The mail!

Peter looked up with wide eyes to see a postman in a bright red jacket striding into the delicatessen, looking only slightly dryer than they did. The man undid a rain flap that covered his shoulder bag and fished out a damp handful of mail. Henrik nearly tackled the man to keep him from leaving.

"Excuse me, Mr. Postman, sir," Henrik blurted out. The tall man gave them a concerned look as he passed his handful of mail across the counter to the deli clerk.

"You kids look like three drowned mice," he told them.

Henrik cleared his throat. "We're from Helsingor and we're looking for someone. We were going to ask at the main post office, but it was closed by the time we got into town. Maybe you would know how to find them."

"You're looking for someone?" The postman, a friendly-looking man with soft green eyes and long sideburns, inspected them more closely. He reminded Peter of a doctor examining his patients.

Henrik looked hopeful. "Right. Their name is Torp. They were kind of family friends, but we don't know where they went when they moved."

"Only that they're somewhere here in Hillerod," added Elise, "and that they recently moved here."

The mail carrier nodded again and scratched his chin. "I see. Well, I've been on this route for the past ten years. There's no Torp here on Main Street."

Henrik only stared, his hair dripping down over his eyes. For a moment, he looked as if he might burst out crying.

"I'm sorry," said the postman in a cheery tone. "You're serious about this, aren't you?"

The man looked through the mail in his bag, muttering to

himself. "Torp, Torp. Sounds kind of familiar . . . maybe . . ."

"You know them?" asked Henrik, once again hopeful.

"I didn't say that." The postman kept searching. "Only that it might . . ."

The man stopped and pulled out a single envelope. "Here it is . . . Torp. Of course, I don't know if it's the Torp you're looking for."

Henrik hopped up and down. "What's the first name? Does it say the address?"

The postman smiled patiently at them. "No first name on the letter. But the address is 38 Mill Street."

Henrik backed away toward the door. "Where's that?"

"Three blocks down that way." The postman pointed. "Left one block. That's Mill Street. Then to the end."

"Fantastic!" yelled Henrik, pulling open the door. "Thanks, mister. I *knew* we'd find them. I just *knew* it."

"But, Henrik," said Elise. "How do we know it's the right Torp?"

Henrik ignored the question. "Are you two coming?" he called back over his shoulder.

Peter felt the warmth from the store chased away by a cold, wet blast from outside.

"Here we go again," sighed Elise. "And I was just starting to dry out."

This time Henrik led the way through the darkness, past brightly lit shops with Christmas decorations of pine boughs and red-suited paper elves peering around the corners. Peter thought they looked dry and warm inside their shop windows.

"Almost there," said Henrik as he skipped round a corner. "Mill Street."

Peter looked back at the brighter lights of the busy street behind them. Mill Street, like several others, branched off from the main street full of stores. "I still can't believe we would run into someone who knows the people we're looking for."

"*If* they're the right Torps," replied Elise. "But we'd better call Mom and tell her what's going on."

Peter's side hurt. "Slow down for a minute, will you, Henrik?"

"We're almost there. I can see the house at the end of the street."

The house at the end of Mill Street was exactly like all the other houses on Mill Street: a cute, square, yellow brick cottage with a red tile roof and a neat postage-stamp yard surrounded by a white picket fence. There was a light on inside, but the shades were drawn. Henrik hurdled over the fence and was already knocking on the front door when Elise and Peter carefully opened the gate to follow.

RACE FOR THE BOOK

"I'm sorry," said a tall man in the doorway. "Catch your breath, and I'll be able to understand what you're saying."

He was younger than their parents, with a wide, smiling face and powerful-looking broad shoulders. His big hand squeezed the life out of a newspaper. Even from a distance, Peter was sure it was the same man who had stayed in Henrik's apartment while the Melchior family was in Sweden.

"Ole, who's there?" came a young woman's voice from somewhere inside.

"It's a boy, Gerta," he replied. "Looks like he's been out in the rain too long. Come here and help me figure out what he wants."

"Don't make him stand there," replied the woman. "Ask him to come inside if he's wet."

But the big man stepped back in surprise when Peter and Elise stepped out of the shadows into the yellow pool of light on the front porch. He squinted his eyes and bent down to take a closer look at their faces as Peter slipped off the hood from his yellow slicker.

"Do I know you kids from somewhere?" he asked, pulling the door open wider.

"Ole, you're letting in all the cold air," scolded the woman, stepping up behind him. "Aren't you going to . . ."

Mrs. Torp was tall enough to look over his shoulder, though Peter was relieved to notice that she wasn't as powerful-looking or broad-shouldered as her husband. Her hair was cropped short, and she wore a comfortable-looking, baggy beige sweater and the same curious, friendly look as the man's.

"It's the Andersen twins from Helsingor, Ole," she finally gasped. "And they're soaked."

"I thought you looked familiar," he said with a smile as he pulled them into the welcome warmth of the cozy house. "But I couldn't figure out where I'd seen you two before." Henrik and the twins stood dripping in the front entry. Peter felt like a fish that had just been caught.

"We're sorry to just show up like this," Peter apologized. "But we're here with our friend Henrik Melchior." He turned to Henrik, who was taking off his coat.

"Henrik . . ." Ole hesitated for a minute as he put out his giant hand for Henrik to shake. "Do I finally meet the Henrik Melchior in whose apartment Gerta and I stayed?"

Henrik nodded shyly and smiled. "That was our place, I guess."

Peter was glad it wasn't his arm Ole was pumping, but Henrik managed to grin and hang on.

"Henrik Melchior," repeated Gerta, as if saying the name for the first time in her life. "Well, of all the people, you're our second visitors here in Hillerod. Welcome to our little house."

There wasn't much room for furniture in the small sitting room next to the kitchen: three painted white bookshelves, a worn, brown corduroy sofa, and a matching brown easy chair with the stuffing coming out of one of the arms. Mostly there were boxes of books piled against the walls.

Gerta settled them around an old kitchen table, where they sat on upside-down boxes and sipped from steaming hot mugs of tea loaded with sugar and milk. Peter closed his eyes and smiled as he felt the hot tea warm him up from the inside out, letting Elise and Henrik do most of the talking, explaining why they had come and how they were searching for Henrik's book.

Sitting on the kitchen counter, Ole looked like a giant teddy bear leaning over to hear their story. Gerta sipped tea and listened with wide eyes, once in a while giving her husband a worried glance.

"Is something wrong?" Elise finally asked.

Gerta caught her breath. "I'm just sorry you had to go to all that trouble to find us."

"Especially since it was all for nothing," added Ole, looking worried.

"Nothing?" asked Henrik hopefully. "What about all these books? You don't think maybe it got packed by mistake?"

The Torps both shook their heads and looked at each other.

"Well, uh, actually it did. . . ." began Ole.

Gerta nodded seriously. "Yes, but it looks like someone already beat you to it."

"What?" Henrik's jaw dropped. "You're not serious."

Gerta nodded again. "He was such a nice fellow. Came by earlier today. Told us the same thing you did about the book from your father. Only . . ."

"Matthias was here?" interrupted Henrik.

"That was his name," replied Gerta. "Matthias Karlsson. Said he was a friend of your father's."

"But why would he come here without telling us?" wondered Peter.

Gerta shook her head and held up her hands. "I'm very sorry. He didn't say anything about you kids coming here this afternoon, or we surely wouldn't have given him the book. He didn't seem to know anything at all about you kids coming."

"And you gave him the book? Just like that?" Henrik still couldn't believe it.

"It was a very old book," explained Ole, holding out his hands to show the size. "Stiff black cover, written all in Hebrew. You know that kind of lettering?"

"With some envelopes stuck between the pages," finished Henrik.

Ole nodded.

"Henrik," said Elise, "it's not that big a deal. We'll just go back home and get it."

Henrik picked up a couple of books from the box next to him. "But . . ."

"Look," Elise continued. "I'm sure Matthias was just trying to do you a favor by getting it for you."

"Right," added Peter. "It was just a mix-up."

Elise nodded her agreement. "All we have to do is call our parents on the phone. We'll find out exactly what happened to the book, and we need to tell Mom and Dad where we are, anyway."

Henrik didn't look convinced.

"That's a good idea," said Gerta. "Ole, why don't you take Henrik next door to use the phone before the kids' parents send the police out to look for them."

"Right." Ole slipped off the counter and patted Henrik on the shoulder. For such a large man, he moved with surprising speed. "Come on, Henrik. We've been using the neighbor's phone until we get one."

While Henrik followed Ole next door to call home, Elise pulled a couple of books out of a box next to the table. Despite the mess, each box had been carefully labeled with a heavy pencil. Several said "Accounting Books," a few said "Novels," and a few more said "Bible Books."

"It may not look like it," smiled Gerta, pointing in the direction of the tallest stack of boxes, "but we like books. Our friends give them to us—kind of like some people get stray kittens left on their doorsteps. We get books."

Elise smiled. "I like books."

"She's always reading about three at a time," Peter explained.

"Me too," replied Gerta. "I'm just glad we didn't have to drag them all to Bornholm Island."

The twins both looked puzzled.

"Ole has family there," continued Gerta. "A second cousin who runs the Mission Hotel, and he wanted Ole to come help him."

"But you came here instead?" asked Peter.

Gerta nodded. "It wasn't a good time to go to the island, since the Russians invaded Bornholm, and then Ole got a good job here in Hillerod. After we moved out of the Melchiors' apartment, we stayed with some friends for a while. . . ." Her voice trailed off. "But I'm sure you didn't come here to hear our life story."

"That's okay." Elise put down the book she had been leafing through. "Are you sure you're going to have enough shelves here?"

Gerta laughed, and the gentle sound made Peter smile.

"We never have enough shelves. We make tables and chairs out of the books that don't fit."

Ole and Henrik came stomping in through the front door just then, followed by another blast of cold air. Gerta looked at them, and her eyebrows were two question marks. Henrik's dark eyes were flashing, and he looked ready to cry.

"We've got to get home right away!" he announced.

"What?" asked Peter.

"Did you get through to the Andersens?" Gerta asked her husband.

Ole nodded and shut the door behind him. "I talked to Peter's dad. They can stay here for dinner and for the night, since there's not another bus tonight. I promised to put them on the first bus in the morning."

He looked over at Henrik, who was standing by the front window of the little house with his arms crossed, looking worried.

"We couldn't get through to Henrik's mom," continued Ole. "The line was busy the whole time."

"So what's the emergency, Henrik?" asked Peter.

Henrik paced back to the kitchen table. "Your dad told us he heard my mom was going to Sweden with Matthias in his airplane."

"Oh," replied Elise. "I thought by the way you were talking

that something bad had happened. What's so terrible about that?"

She stopped when she saw the dark expression on Henrik's face.

"When are they leaving?" asked Peter.

Henrik shrugged. "Your dad thought tomorrow morning, first thing, as long as the weather is good."

"You probably need to talk to her yourself then," replied Peter. "Are you going to try again?"

Ole nodded and kept his coat on. "We'll go back and try in a couple of minutes. Right, Henrik?"

Henrik nodded. "I hope it keeps raining so they can't fly."

Gerta looked from the twins to Henrik. "I take it this Matthias fellow is not one of Henrik's favorite folks," she whispered to Elise.

Elise shook her head and whispered back. "We try not to mention the subject."

Twenty minutes later, Ole and Henrik returned through the front door.

"Well, did you find out about your book, Henrik?" asked Peter.

Henrik shook his head and sat down, looking defeated. "My mom said she didn't know anything about it, but she'd ask when she saw Matthias. She was in a hurry."

"Oh." Peter wasn't sure how to end the conversation. They had spent all afternoon looking for Henrik's book, and now there really wasn't anything left to do or say about it. He looked over at Elise for help.

"Well, I think that's exciting," chirped Elise. "Flying to Sweden for a visit. Maybe they'll take you for a ride sometime, do you think?"

Henrik seemed to consider the prospect, and Peter thought he saw a glimmer in his friend's eye. He knew from all the times they had spent talking about flying in an airplane that the thought must have crossed Henrik's mind.

"When is your mother coming back?" asked Gerta.

"Tomorrow night," replied Henrik. "They're just going for the day. But she's leaving tomorrow morning early, so she won't be there when we get back."

"I'm sure she'll be fine." Gerta poured Henrik another cup of steaming tea.

Henrik nodded his head. An unexpected grin started to play on the corner of his mouth. He sighed, closed his eyes, and nodded again. "Yeah. I guess that would be kind of fun sometime. Maybe."

MYSTERIOUS
PHONE CALL

"I know," Henrik agreed once more after dinner the next day, back home in the Andersen apartment. "They were really nice people." He looked up at the clock. It was almost six-thirty.

"Well, I'm just glad you found them when you did," said Mrs. Andersen, helping to stack dishes. "I was starting to worry about you kids, being out there in the rain all afternoon."

Peter looked up nervously at the clock, the same way Henrik had, then glanced through the wide entry that connected their kitchen and living rooms. From his spot by the sink, he could see the bare Christmas tree set up in a bucket near the middle of the floor. Mr. Andersen and Grandfather Andersen were wrestling with the tree, trying to make it stand up straight.

"Arne, don't you think you should call somebody?" Mrs. Andersen suggested. "They said they would be back from Sweden before it was dark. It's been almost three hours. . . ."

Mr. Andersen grunted from behind the tree as he tried to tilt it from below. "Who would I call?" he answered. "We don't even know where they went in Sweden."

"I'm sure they'll call us if anything is wrong," added Grandfather. He steadied the tree from above. "I understand this Karlsson fellow is a good pilot."

While the two men were struggling with the tree, Elise tiptoed into the living room, picked out a woven paper heart from a box on the sofa, and tried to hang it up on a branch.

"Caught you!" teased Grandfather Andersen with a twinkle in his eye.

"Oh, Grandfather," said Elise. "Don't you think we could help decorate the tree this year? We're old enough."

"You know the tradition." He smiled back at her. "Parents decorate. Kids get to see the tree after it's done. You wouldn't go peeking at your Christmas presents, now, would you?"

Elise giggled as Tiger pounced on a little box of paper decorations that was sitting on the floor.

"Cats don't help, either!" insisted Grandfather, rescuing the box of flags and angels. "Now, shoo!"

Elise retreated to where Peter was now standing in the wide entry that joined the kitchen and living rooms.

"I guess we know when we're not wanted," Peter joked.

"You shouldn't even be watching," complained Grandfather, still smiling. "When I was your age, my parents shut the doors of the parlor—we didn't even get a peek at the tree until everything was decorated and the candles lit. That's the tradition."

"Arne," warned Mrs. Andersen from the kitchen sink, "you're going to have a bucket of water nearby if we light any of those candles on the tree, aren't you?"

Mr. Andersen laughed. "Don't you worry. We're not going to burn anything down. Dad, hand me some more of those flags, would you, please?"

Tiger was waiting behind the sofa for the string of flags, and when Grandfather Andersen began to untangle them, he pounced.

"Hey, you!" said Grandfather, yanking the flags out of the cat's reach and waving them high in the air. "We don't need your help, thank you." Tiger reared up on his hind legs and swiped at the decorations.

"Come on, Tiger." Peter laughed and picked up his cat. "I don't think you and I are appreciated around here anymore. How about a nice snack?" He lowered Tiger gently to the floor and refilled the cat's milk bowl from a pitcher on the table.

Henrik still sat at the kitchen table, staring straight ahead. Peter bent down and waved his hand in front of his friend's face.

"Hello in there," said Peter. "Anybody home?"

Henrik shook his head and stood up quickly. "Thanks for the good dinner, Mrs. Andersen."

"Dinner's been over for fifteen minutes, Henrik," Peter pointed out.

"Peter!" scolded Mrs. Andersen. Then her voice softened. "You're very welcome, Henrik. And don't you worry. I'm sure your mother will be back any minute, or else she'll call."

"Mom," asked Elise, "don't you think we can help decorate the tree this year?"

Mrs. Andersen wiped her hands on her apron. "You know what your father said. . . ."

"Aw, but that's not fair," said Peter.

"You'll see it when it's done," interrupted Grandfather Andersen, overhearing their conversation. "This is what dads do on Little Christmas Eve."

"Moms too," said Mrs. Andersen, slipping out to the living room to help.

Little Christmas Eve. The night of December 23. Next to Christmas Eve itself, Little Christmas Eve was one of the most exciting times of the Christmas season in Denmark. Mr. and Mrs. Andersen decorated the tree while the kids wrapped presents and generally got excited. Peter took a deep breath to smell one of his favorite smells: fresh-cut fir. Then he took up his post once more between the kitchen and living rooms, where he could see everything.

"It seems like we ought to be doing something," mumbled Henrik, staring at the phone in the kitchen.

"Why don't you boys help Elise with her cookies?" suggested

Mrs. Andersen, looking for a branch on which to hang a little elf made of red yarn.

Peter looked back at Henrik, who was still sitting at the kitchen table. "Mom, I don't think he meant that kind of doing something."

"I know what he meant," she replied, "but maybe this would help take your minds off worrying. There's simply nothing we can do right now."

A knock at the door launched Henrik out of the kitchen to the front entryway.

"Merry Little Christmas Eve!" came Uncle Morten's cheery greeting.

"We came to help decorate the tree," echoed Aunt Lisbeth, sounding every bit as merry. "And I smell something good!"

"Cookies, Lisbeth," Elise chimed in. "I mean, *Aunt* Lisbeth."

Lisbeth smiled. "Oh, that's okay. I keep forgetting, too."

Even though the wedding was months ago, Peter and Elise were still just getting used to calling Lisbeth "Aunt." And she was still just getting used to hearing it. She stepped into the kitchen, dressed for the holidays in a dark green ankle-length skirt and striped red-and-gold sweater. Her dark, curly hair was tied back in a ponytail with a bright holiday ribbon.

Henrik followed the couple into the kitchen, his glum look the complete opposite of Morten's and Lisbeth's happy smiles.

"Good thing we showed up when we did," said the broad-shouldered Uncle Morten, giving the twins a puzzled smile as he set down a bag of groceries on the kitchen counter. When he grinned, his pearly white teeth seemed to shine from behind his blond beard, and his cheeks were rosy red from the cold outside. "This party looks like it needs some livening up."

He looked down at Henrik, who stood awkwardly by the window, staring outside.

"Did I do something wrong already?" asked Uncle Morten.

"Merry Christmas, you two." Mrs. Andersen stepped in from the living room to explain. "We were waiting for Henrik's mother to get back. She went up with their friend Matthias Karlsson in his airplane, and they were supposed to be back before dark."

"Oh, well, it's still only . . ." Morten looked down at his wrist-watch and his voice trailed off. "It's six-forty."

No one said anything for a minute, and Uncle Morten cleared his throat nervously. "Well, this calls for something special, don't you think, Arne?" he asked, looking into the living room.

"What's that?" asked Mr. Andersen.

"Uh . . ." stammered Uncle Morten, looking at Lisbeth for help. She looked at the twins and smiled.

"I think all the kids should be able to help decorate the tree this year," she announced, but then she put her hand to her cheek. "Oh, Henrik, I forgot about you not celebrating Christmas. It's just that . . ."

Henrik shook his head. "It's okay, I don't mind. Mother will be back any minute. I'll . . . uh, maybe I'll just watch."

"I'm not so sure about changing tradition," said Grandfather Andersen from behind the tall tree. "Kids are supposed to wait until the father decorates the tree."

"Kids are supposed to have fun at Christmas," said Lisbeth, stepping into the living room and picking up a paper decoration. It looked like an ice-cream cone made out of bright foil with a little handle across the top. When Peter peeked out into the living room, he saw his father filling the cones with little pieces of licorice, raisins, or nuts.

Mr. Andersen, like everyone else in the family, had a hard time saying no to Lisbeth.

"Well, maybe just this once," he said, hanging another cone on the tree. It bowed from the weight, and Peter made a mental note to remember that cone.

The tree was as tall as their father, or even Uncle Morten. By that time, there was already a star at the top and several strings of bright red-and-white Danish flags draped across the branches, as well as a few woven paper hearts and little golden drums. Several white candles with weighted brass holders were clipped to the stronger branches.

"But you kids keep away from the goodies," warned Mr. Andersen as Peter and Elise pranced into the living room to help.

Peter nodded seriously as he chewed a bite of black, salty licorice he had discovered in one of the decorations. "Absolutely, Dad. This is my last piece."

Mr. Andersen laughed and turned back to the tree while Elise found a couple of records in brown paper covers for their small record player in the corner of the living room. Lisbeth pulled up a kitchen chair so she could reach the upper branches.

"This tree needs a woman's touch, don't you think, Elise?" she asked, hanging a red elf made of yarn.

Elise laughed her approval and turned on the player. The song reminded Peter of some of the other happy Christmas times he had spent with his family. Times when the air was filled with the sound of a choir singing "Silent Night" and the warm, buttery smell of Elise's cookies. Peter forgot what he had told his father earlier and popped another bite of licorice into his mouth. As he helped Lisbeth with a tinsel string, he glanced back at the kitchen. Henrik was still camped by the telephone, looking like a puppy waiting for its meal.

"Peter, what about that licorice?" warned his father. But Mr. Andersen was grinning as he pointed at Peter. "No reason to get a stomachache before tomorrow."

Peter swallowed his candy. "Sorry, Dad."

An hour later, the tree was almost decorated, and Peter followed his nose into the kitchen. "Time for a taste test," he announced. "Henrik, do you want a cookie, too?"

Henrik had slouched down in his chair, crossed his arms, and was resting his chin on his chest. He didn't move until the ring of the phone made him jerk.

"I'll get it," said Peter, jumping for the phone on its little table in the kitchen. A quick glance at the clock on the wall told him it was eight o'clock.

"I'm sure that's probably your mother, Henrik," said Mrs. Andersen in a reassuring tone.

"Yeah, I'm sure it's your mom," echoed Elise.

"But if you don't answer the phone, we'll never find out," added Grandfather Andersen.

Peter lifted the receiver carefully, only to be hit by a storm of crackles and pops. He held the receiver back from his ear and motioned for Elise to join him. Henrik also leaned close.

"Andersen residence," said Peter, not at all sure if anyone would be able to hear him.

A wave of static seemed to wash through the telephone, and the three of them waited. The rest of the family looked curiously into the kitchen.

"Hello?" Peter said once again, and this time he thought he heard a faint voice on the other end.

"Ronne on the island of Bornholm" came a man's voice, or maybe a boy's. He sounded as if he were talking faintly through the end of a tube, and there was something very different about the voice.

"I'm sorry, I can't hear what you're saying," yelled Peter. "We have a bad connection."

More static. Henrik leaned closer.

"I think he said he's calling from Bornholm," reported Elise, straining to hear more. "Can you understand him?"

Peter shook his head. Bornholm! Someone else had recently mentioned the island, but who was it? He couldn't understand what was being said, either, but he guessed maybe that was because of the speaker's Bornholm accent—if that's what it was. Peter knew that people on the little Danish island of Bornholm had their own peculiar brand of Danish, one that most Danes had a hard time understanding. The island, after all, was miles away from the mainland, far out in the Baltic Sea.

Then it came to him: Ole and Gerta Torp had said something about the island. Something about a relative who worked at the Mission Hotel. But the memory was as fuzzy as the voice they were trying to hear. Then the static faded, and Peter heard the voice much more clearly.

"I said, I'm calling from the island of Bornholm" came the foreign-sounding voice once more. "And I have a message for you from someone named Matthias Karlsson."

Peter covered the mouthpiece with his hand. "He says there's a message from Matthias!"

By that time, the adults had crowded into the kitchen. Mr. Andersen took the phone but still held it out as Peter had so the rest of them could hear.

"This is Arne Andersen," boomed Peter's father. "What's the message?"

The wave of static rolled in once more, and they couldn't hear anything else.

"Could you repeat what you just said?" asked Mr. Andersen. "We're all the way over here in Helsingor."

"Okay, listen" came the voice once more, this time a little clearer and louder. "But you must promise not to tell anyone you received this call. Do I have your word?"

Everyone in the kitchen seemed to hold their breath. Tiger jumped up on the table in the middle of the crowd, and Mrs. Andersen quickly swept him off.

"Of course," replied Peter's father. "But why—"

"Never mind," interrupted the strange voice. He could have been calling from the moon, he sounded so far away. "Karlsson landed on the island today in a small plane." There was a pause. "Are you there?"

"I hear you now," replied Mr. Andersen.

"Good, because if he is your friend, he will need your help."

"What kind of help?"

"He's suspected of being a spy and will be taken to Moscow unless . . ." The voice faded out once more.

"Wait a minute," yelled Mr. Andersen over the static. "What are you saying?"

"I said, if he's a friend of yours, and you want to see him again, I would get over here and try to free him."

"Where is he?"

"Locked up. That's all I can tell you."

Peter looked around at the shocked expressions on everyone's faces.

"Who do we speak to?" shouted Mr. Andersen.

"Ivanov. Captain Ivanov. But he's hard to deal with, and he won't listen to just anyone. I can't tell you anything else."

"Wait a minute, don't hang up! Was there a woman, too? Shorter, with dark hair and dark eyes . . ."

The connection became fuzzy once again, and everyone moved closer to hear the answer.

" . . . woman . . . her head . . . hurt."

"What? Did you say she hurt her head?" Mr. Andersen shouted into the phone.

There were more pops and scratches and a couple of sounds that could have been words. Peter closed his eyes to hear better, then gave up.

Elise straightened up. "He said 'hurt,' I think."

Mr. Andersen put a finger to his lips and closed one eye, still listening. But by that time, all they could hear was a warbling, whistling sound, like a hurricane in a box. Peter kept listening, hopeful, but after a couple of minutes, Grandfather shook his head.

"I think that's all we're going to hear," he said.

"You can hang up, Arne," agreed Uncle Morten.

Henrik ran a hand through his hair and looked around the room as Peter's father gently replaced the black telephone receiver.

"Is he going to call back?" asked Henrik.

Uncle Morten shook his head. "I don't think so. But at least it sounds like your mother is safe."

"We don't know that," replied Henrik, crossing his arms. "But I'm going to go find out."

"Okay, slow down." Peter's father paced across the kitchen floor. "You can't do anything alone. Wait for a couple of minutes to see if this fellow calls back. Then if he doesn't, we can make some calls of our own to see what's going on."

"He never even told us his name," said Henrik.

Elise retreated to the living room, where the record player was still stuck on the end of the record they had on since before the phone call. Peter and Henrik wandered out with her while the adults talked to each other around the kitchen table in serious voices.

"Wow, can you believe it?" asked Peter, lifting the arm of the record player and turning it off. Henrik peeked into the kitchen to watch the phone.

"I don't think he's going to call back," said Henrik after a few minutes.

"I think you're right," agreed Mr. Andersen. "I'm going to make a few calls of our own."

Peter's father began dialing while Henrik and the twins paced the kitchen floor. But with each call, Peter grew more and more discouraged.

"Can't you try again?" Mr. Andersen asked the phone operator on the fifth call. "There must be some way to get through to the island. This is urgent."

More pacing.

"I understand what you're saying. But if none of the lines are working from here to there, how was someone able to call us? No, operator, I don't have that number. I don't even know the name of the fellow who called."

Mr. Andersen finally hung up the phone in disgust.

"I don't know who else to call." He threw up his hands. "The operator can't help us, the police say it's a local matter, and everyone says no one can do anything as long as the Russians are still occupying Bornholm. There aren't even any ferries running until next week because of the holidays."

Henrik slammed his hand down on the table. "What is it with those Russians? I don't understand what they're doing on Bornholm, anyway. Who invited them?"

"They got the Germans to surrender when they bombed the island," replied Mr. Andersen. "But now they won't go home, and I don't think the islanders can tell much difference between them and the Nazis."

"Well, I'm not going to just sit here while my mom needs

help," replied Henrik, getting up from the table. "She could be hurt bad."

Mrs. Andersen put her hand on Henrik's shoulder and looked over at her husband. "Isn't there something else we can do, Arne?"

"What about taking the *Anna Marie* over?" Peter suggested excitedly. "We know someone over there."

"Who?" Mrs. Andersen looked at him with a question on her face.

"Oh, I remember," said Elise. "Ole Torp's cousin, right? At one of the hotels there."

Peter nodded. "Right."

Everyone looked at Uncle Morten, who was standing in the doorway to the living room, tugging thoughtfully at his beard.

"I could have the boat ready to sail in a couple of hours. The weather's still not too good, but we should be able to make it down to Bornholm in a day or so."

Peter looked back excitedly at his father. "Then can we—"

"Don't even think about it," interrupted Mr. Andersen. "If we can't get through to anyone on the phone in the morning, and if your uncle takes the boat, it certainly won't be with any kids aboard."

"But remember the guy on the phone said we should do everything we can to help show them Matthias is not a spy?" suggested Elise.

"Tomorrow is Christmas Eve," replied Mr. Andersen. "And you're not going. Period."

A COLD WELCOME

"Keep it heading south, southeast," commanded Uncle Morten. He peered out through the front window of the *Anna Marie*, looked down at the compass, and kept his hand on Peter's shoulder.

"South, southeast," repeated Peter, the way his uncle had once taught them. Elise was sleeping in the small bunk compartment behind the large wooden steering wheel while Henrik was keeping watch. No one had said much since they left the harbor at Helsingor early that Christmas Eve morning.

This is going to be one of the strangest Christmases ever, Peter said to himself.

When he looked over, Henrik was still chewing on the same piece of gum he had started five hours earlier, and he was still looking outside at the waves. With a strong wind from behind, Peter could feel the waves pick up the little fishing boat, and he had to struggle to keep the back end of the boat from swinging out too far.

"Feels like we're doing a little surfing here," commented Uncle Morten. He checked his watch. "At least we're making good time. We should make Bornholm by dinnertime."

"Aye-aye, skipper." Peter gave his uncle a salute.

"Watch out there, Peter. Don't make me sorry I convinced your parents to let you kids come along."

Peter nodded. "We won't, Uncle Morten. We won't be any trouble."

"That's what I told them," answered Uncle Morten. "And I'm counting on it, because to tell you the truth, I'm not sure I know why your parents let me take you along—especially on Christmas."

Peter shrugged. "Henrik was pretty stubborn, remember? And you told them it's probably just some misunderstanding. Having kids along would help soften up the situation."

"I said that?" Uncle Morten grinned.

"And besides, Mom promised she would save the Christmas goose until we all got back. She's worried about Henrik's mom, too."

"I don't think there's anything to worry about, Henrik." Uncle Morten shook his head and looked in Henrik's direction. "Like I told Peter's folks, we'll be on our way home with your mother and Matthias before you know it."

"You think it will be that easy?" Henrik didn't sound so sure.

Uncle Morten cleared his throat. "These aren't the Germans we'll be dealing with. They have no right to hold a Dane and a Swede if the people have done nothing. We'll get this cleared up in a hurry."

Peter's mind began to wander as they continued to push through gray waves topped with white foam. While the powerful little engine kept its own *chug-cough* rhythm, he couldn't help thinking back to the odd phone call that had launched their trip.

"If you want to see him again . . ." The caller's voice seemed to ring inside Peter's head. *"I would get over here and try to free him."*

"We're going to find them, Henrik," said Peter softly. He knew the engine noise made it impossible for Henrik to hear him, but he said it anyway. "We're going to find your mom, and we're going to find Matthias, and we're going to find those letters of your dad's. We're going to find out what they say."

Uncle Morten looked at his nephew curiously. "Are you talking to yourself, Peter?"

Peter just shook his head and grinned as a wave jolted them from behind. Elise raised her head from the bunk, looked at them, and blinked. There was barely enough room for her to sit up in the little cubbyhole Uncle Morten had built into the back of the wheelhouse. Her mouth moved, but Peter couldn't hear anything.

"I said," she repeated loudly, "Are we there yet?"

"Not yet," repeated Uncle Morten, loud enough for everyone to hear. "It'll be a few more hours."

Elise felt around her pillow, pulled back, and screeched.

"There's something alive in there!" she hollered, jumping out and bumping into Peter at the wheel.

"What are you doing, Elise?" he asked. "You're dreaming."

Henrik stuck his head into the shadowy sleeping compartment, reached in, and pulled out a wiggling ball of fur.

"Your cat, Peter," he said, holding up Tiger for all of them to see.

"Tiger!" Peter reached out and took the surprised animal. "What are you doing here?"

Uncle Morten looked up and groaned. "Just what we need. Peter's tagalong cat. What are you going to do with him?"

"We'll take care of him, Uncle Morten," replied Peter. Tiger looked nervously around at all the water, as if he had just woken up. "We'll keep him on the boat."

Uncle Morten shook his head. "But what about—"

"We'll tear up some paper and make him a litter box," put in Elise.

"Thanks, sis," Peter whispered. "Good idea."

Uncle Morten frowned and looked ahead, then behind them. "Well, it's a sure thing that we can't turn around now. If anything happens to that animal, though, don't be disappointed."

"We'll keep him inside," promised Peter, holding Tiger up to his face. "He won't be any trouble, right, Tiger?"

Peter knew that the island of Bornholm was different from the rest of Denmark. Their teacher at school had told them it was hilly, rocky, and full of thick woods. The rest of the country was flat and full of farms and villages.

"We just passed that light there, see?" Uncle Morten pointed to a number on the chart he had spread out on a little shelf in front of the steering wheel—what would be a dashboard in a car. "Keep to the left, and look for the next one. That will take us into the harbor."

Peter was still steering, but he tightened his grip on the steering wheel and leaned forward as far as he could. Henrik was at his side, Elise on the other, looking for lights. Tiger had quickly gotten used to the waves and was keeping watch from his own perch next to the map.

"I see it!" announced Elise. "Straight ahead of us."

"I see it, too," added Peter, easing the wheel to the right. A moment later, they slipped by the dark shape of a buoy, topped like a Christmas tree with a blinking green light. Peter was glad the wind had settled down.

"If we're on the right course, we should be able to see the lights of the city of Ronne by now," said Uncle Morten, checking his chart once more.

Peter looked out ahead but could see nothing. *What if we're in the wrong place?*

A couple more minutes passed with no one saying a word, as everyone just stared out through the front window. Henrik slipped outside onto the side deck for a better look but returned quickly.

"Too cold out there," he said, blowing on his hands. The engine just below their feet was loud, but at least it helped keep them toasty.

"This is strange," said Uncle Morten. "Every time I've been to Ronne before, I've been able to see lights. This time there's nothing. Like they're still keeping everything dark, same way we had to do during the war."

"You've been here before?" asked Peter.

"Years ago," replied their uncle. "Before the war."

They all stared a few minutes longer, until finally Peter thought he could see a smudge of light ahead. "Is that what we're looking for?" he asked, pointing.

As they crept through the still, dark waters, they could see a few outlines of buildings in the distance, lights in houses, and the harbor entrance lights. Uncle Morten nodded in the strange glow of the red light from their compass.

"The harbor's just like back home in Helsingor," Uncle Morten told them. "We'll steer straight through those lights up ahead, then keep right. I'll take it after that."

Peter was glad to give the steering wheel back to his uncle as they crept into the strange harbor.

"I thought it was Christmas," said Elise, studying the dim lights and shadowy buildings. One of them—a large, older warehouse—looked like a dark, ghostly ruin.

"What happened to that place?" asked Henrik.

"Same thing that happened to the rest of this city," replied Uncle Morten, steering for a lineup of what looked like fishing boats. "When the Germans wouldn't give up at the end of the war, the Russians came in and bombed it flat. With friends like that, who needs enemies, right?"

As they drew closer to the pier, Peter could see other buildings that looked as if they had been hit by bombs. Some had tarps wrapped around them; others were partly rebuilt.

"Wow, look at that one, Elise," said Peter. "Looks like the roof just came off."

"We'll have a chance to do some sightseeing in the morning," Uncle Morten told them. "Right now we need to get tied up and find a place to stay."

Elise shivered and folded her arms. "This place gives me the creeps."

"Me too," agreed Peter. "I knew some of the houses were

bombed, but I didn't know it would look this bad."

Peter pulled up his collar and stepped out on deck with Henrik as Uncle Morten pulled the *Anna Marie* into a space between another fishing boat and a small tugboat. They would tie up just opposite the brick warehouse building with the big holes in the roof.

"Watch where you're stepping," warned Uncle Morten.

As soon as their boat bumped softly against the side of the pier, the boys each jumped out with a mooring line into the darkness, Henrik in the front and Peter in the back. As quickly as he could, Peter twisted his rope into a figure eight around the wings of a large iron cleat.

"Does that look okay, Uncle Morten?" Peter asked when a tall shadow appeared over where he was finishing tying his knot. But there was no answer, and when Peter straightened up, he was staring at the dark figure of a soldier pointing a rifle at him.

Unknown Friends

Even in the darkness, Peter could tell that the soldier was big. The man towered over Peter like a gorilla defending his territory. He wore a wool jacket and a winter cap with fur ear flaps, like the ones Peter had seen Russian soldiers wearing in newsreels at the movies.

"Uncle Morten?" Peter called just as the *Anna Marie*'s engine shut down. "Uncle Morten, I need you out here."

Uncle Morten popped his head out of the side door as a group of flashlights came bouncing down the pier toward them. Uncle Morten saw the soldier, too, and slipped over to where Peter stood frozen.

"Is there a problem with us tying up here?" asked Uncle Morten, standing between Peter and the big guard.

The man pulled his rifle up only slightly and seemed to puff up his chest at Uncle Morten. He looked over his shoulder at the lights coming their way.

"*Ya ni panimayou,*" said the soldier in his own language. Whatever that meant, Peter didn't want to move, so he held on to Uncle Morten's belt loop and shivered in the darkness.

A moment later, Peter squinted at the white light in his face as three powerful flashlights lit up the *Anna Marie*. Elise huddled inside the wheelhouse, and Henrik had climbed back on as well. The air was filled with more strange Russian words, a language which to Peter sounded like someone talking backward with a mouth full of food. All he could tell was that one of the men with the flashlights was asking the first guard questions; another man had a clipboard and was taking notes as he studied their boat. They were all dressed in the same drab coats and fur hats.

"Did we land in the right country?" Peter whispered to his uncle. Uncle Morten put his hand on Peter's shoulder.

Uncle Morten cleared his throat. "Does anyone here speak Danish?"

The men didn't answer, but the first guard, the man Peter thought was as big as a gorilla, kept his rifle ready.

"English?" Uncle Morten tried once more. The men continued talking among themselves. "German?"

Uncle Morten's last question finally got their attention. The one who seemed to be in charge, a man who looked a few years older than the other two, stared straight at Uncle Morten while he waved at the others to inspect the boat. Elise and Henrik crawled down quickly to where Peter and his uncle stood on the pier before one of the guards pushed into the wheelhouse and looked around.

"What about Tiger?" Elise whispered into Peter's ear.

Peter looked back at the boat and tried to think where they had left the cat. If he escaped here on the strange island, they might never find him again.

"Hey, my cat," said Peter, climbing back on the boat.

"*Nyet*," grunted the man in charge, waving his rifle. Peter froze, then tried to make the shape of a cat with his hands to make the man understand.

"Peter, get back here," ordered Uncle Morten. "The cat is fine."

Peter reluctantly rejoined the others while the guard motioned with his head for them to move. The guard on the boat grabbed Uncle Morten's identification papers and a notebook from a shelf above the steering wheel.

"Careful with those papers," protested Uncle Morten, holding his hand up. The first guard waved his rifle for them to start walking toward the dark town. They had no choice but to obey.

"What do these men want?" asked Elise as they marched.

Uncle Morten looked back at their boat, bobbing safely at the pier. At least the side doors had been slammed shut, and Peter could only hope that Tiger was locked safely inside.

"I don't know, kids," Uncle Morten told them quietly. "But I'm sure it will be fine once we talk with someone who understands us. Right now let's just do as they say."

Peter stayed as close to his uncle as he could.

"Mission Hotel?" Uncle Morten tried once more as they left the pier area.

This time the big guard grunted and seemed to nod, but Peter couldn't tell for sure if any of the soldiers understood a word they said.

"Wow, Peter, look at these houses," whispered Henrik as they walked through the streets of the little city. It might have looked like a hundred other places, but nearly every building was either half blown away or the roof was missing. Others were being repaired, with ladders and timbers still stacked around giant piles of bricks. Very few houses were untouched, though a few had soft lights coming from behind drawn shades.

"Merry Christmas," whispered Peter, and his whisper echoed through the eerie streets.

"We don't even know if the Mission Hotel is still standing," Henrik said.

The soldiers pointed them past a row of completely leveled houses, still just piles of splintered wood. The next block was better; a few buildings even looked as if they had escaped the bombs, though it was hard to tell in the darkness. Then on the corner ahead of them, a two-story brick building with only the corner chipped away stood blazing with light. The soldiers guided them to the front door.

"The Mission Hotel?" asked Henrik, reading a sign over the door. "Hey, this is it!"

"Hot-tell Mizh-zhone," answered the leader, followed by something in Russian and hand signals telling them to go inside. He stood back while Uncle Morten opened the front door of the hotel, and they stepped into the light.

Peter paused as he was greeted by the warm smell of roast pork and red cabbage, laced with heavy cigarette smoke. Groups of young men were clustered around the lobby, playing cards, smoking, laughing, and talking to each other in Russian.

"Where does he want us to go now?" Peter wondered out loud.

The room hushed when they walked in. The young men looked away from their cards long enough to size them up. Peter tried not to look around as they followed Uncle Morten and the guard through a maze of tables and several clouds of smoke. Finally they stood before a man sitting by himself at a small table in the corner of the room.

Their guard saluted nervously, handed over the *Anna Marie's* papers, and rattled off in Russian what Peter took to be an introduction. The man at the table—obviously an officer—looked up casually from his dinner of potatoes and meat swimming in steaming gravy.

His uniform was the same as all the other soldiers'—a stiff, dark green shirt with a high-buttoned collar—except he had stars on his orange-striped shoulder pads and several large medals pinned over his shirt pocket. He smiled at them, displaying a set of crooked, stained teeth that seemed to point in every direction of the compass. Then he put down his fork and motioned for them to sit down.

"You speak Danish?" asked Uncle Morten as they found chairs. Their guard had disappeared.

The officer studied them intently, leaving the question hanging in the smoky air around them as he thumbed through the papers. When he looked up, his piercing brown eyes seemed to bore holes through them, but he was smiling beneath a large black handlebar of a mustache.

"*Pazhalsta*," he answered, putting down the papers and holding up a finger for them to wait. Then he bellowed something into the crowd, sending a couple of men running from their tables.

All this time and still they had not seen any Dane on this strange island, until Peter finally sighted a dark-haired teenager clearing tables. Peter tried to get his attention, but the teenager soon disappeared with an armload of dishes.

Meanwhile, the officer held out cigarettes to Uncle Morten, which Peter's uncle politely refused.

"How are we going to talk with this guy?" Peter whispered to his sister. Around them, the celebrating had started up once more.

"I think we're in Russia," whispered Henrik.

Elise looked around nervously while Uncle Morten tried a little sign language and some slow, loud words.

"Morten Andersen," he announced, pointing to himself.

"*Da*," replied the officer. "Captain Ivanov." He looked impatiently around the room.

"We're looking for his mother," said Uncle Morten, pointing at Henrik. "And—"

The captain nodded, then interrupted with a stream of Russian when he noticed someone coming through the crowd. They turned to see a thin little man, young and dressed in the same uniform as Captain Ivanov, but with only one star on his shoulder.

"I am Lieutenant Riznik," he said, bowing slightly as he edged up to the table and stood behind Captain Ivanov. Each word seemed forced and painful, but at least it was in a language they understood, or close to it. "I serve as Captain Ivanov's translator. You have met?"

"Finally someone who speaks Danish!" sighed Uncle Morten. "Could you tell the captain that—"

Lieutenant Riznik held up his hand as he listened to Captain Ivanov, who gestured at the papers and handed them up for him to look at. Henrik and the twins looked back and forth between the two men, then over at their translator.

"This is going to make me dizzy if we have many conversations like this," Henrik whispered to Peter.

"The captain says that you are required to fill out a landing request in the morning to explain the purpose of your visit," said the young lieutenant.

"Listen," said Uncle Morten, standing up. "I'd be glad to tell you why we're here. In fact, why don't you tell the captain—"

Captain Ivanov cut him off with a rapid-fire command. The officer seemed to smile slightly, then raised his glass to them and nodded for Uncle Morten to sit down.

"The captain insists that you stay with your children for Christmas dinner," said the little man. "Unless, of course, you have other plans."

Uncle Morten sighed and looked at the twins.

"Ask him about my mom," said Henrik.

"What was that?" asked the interpreter, leaning forward. "I did not hear what the young man said. . . ."

Uncle Morten sat down while Captain Ivanov smiled and shouted for what had to be more food.

"Tell your captain thank you for the invitation," said Uncle Morten, twisting a napkin in his hands under the table. "And the boy was asking about an airplane. We're looking for a small, private airplane that landed here on Bornholm some time late yesterday. Actually, we're looking for the pilot and the one passenger. The boy's mother. Can you tell us where they might be?"

Their interpreter translated the question while the captain began eating again. Peter looked behind them, and the busboy he had seen earlier was clearing a table right behind them.

The captain stopped chewing as if he had choked on a piece of meat, then smiled again and mumbled a response. Their interpreter took a step backward and bumped the busboy, almost sending a load of dishes to the floor.

"Excuse me," mumbled the teenager in Danish. He looked

briefly at the twins, picked up a couple more dishes, and hurried away.

Finally the little lieutenant turned back to the table.

"The captain says that you will like the roast chicken."

"Yes, but did you ask him my question?" insisted Uncle Morten.

The interpreter gave them a thin smile. "We have over seven thousand guest troops from the Soviet army staying on your little island. If an airplane had landed, I am sure one of us would have seen it. But of course, it may be possible . . ."

Something about the little man's voice made Peter look more closely. Then he leaned over and whispered in Elise's ear.

"Does something sound familiar about the interpreter's voice?" he asked.

Elise raised her eyebrows. "I don't think so, Peter," she whispered back. "We've never met anyone from Russia before."

Peter frowned. *Elise is right*, he thought.

The captain continued eating, then waved at his interpreter to leave as the same teenager who had carried out dirty dishes came forward with four plates of steaming food.

"Wait a minute," said Uncle Morten to the lieutenant, but the little man merely nodded and left.

"Well, we might as well enjoy the dinner," sighed Uncle Morten. He looked up, and the captain made a stirring motion with his fork in the air.

"*Hlieba kartoshki*," ordered the captain.

"That's the same thing my mom does at home," explained Henrik. "I think it must mean 'eat.' "

Peter looked down at the plate the teenager had brought him. After a day on the water, the food looked and smelled better than anything. He closed his eyes to pray, then heard the sound of silverware dropping on the floor next to his feet.

"Oops," mumbled the teenager. The boy straightened out, but not before Peter felt something stuffed into his shoe.

What's that? wondered Peter, reaching down to fish out a small note. He was on the end of the table, and the captain was waving

at Uncle Morten while Henrik and Elise looked on. No one noticed as Peter unfolded the note in his lap.

I can help you, someone had scrawled in pencil on the back of
a dinner receipt. *Come to the kitchen at eight.*

Peter glanced up at a mantel clock across the room. Seven
forty-five.

A few minutes later, Captain Ivanov finished his meal, rose
from the table, and gestured for Uncle Morten to follow him.
"Riznik!" he bellowed, and once again the interpreter came scur-
rying.

But when Peter and the others tried to follow, the captain
shook his head and told them all to sit once more.

"The captain says he needs to talk alone with Mr. Andersen,"
said Lieutenant Riznik. "You three will wait here."

Elise looked nervous as she glanced around her at the room
full of celebrating soldiers.

"It's okay, kids," said Uncle Morten. "Maybe I can find out
something more about Henrik's mom. I'll meet you back here."

Peter nodded seriously, thinking about the note. As soon as
the men had disappeared into a side room, he unwadded it from
his pocket and showed it to the other two.

"It's almost eight," agreed Henrik. "Let's go see what he
wants."

Peter led the way across the dining room through groups of
soldiers to the back, where a swinging door led to the kitchen.
An older man was washing dishes in the corner, and in the middle, a large black cook stove was piled high with pots full of gravy
and bubbling red cabbage. Without the cigarette smoke from all
the soldiers, it smelled even better than it had out in the dining
room.

"So is that boy going to meet us here?" wondered Henrik.

Peter felt the piece of paper in his pocket. "That's what the
note said, but . . ."

Someone pushed through the door just then, a red-haired girl
about two or three years older than they. Peter had never seen a
girl with so many freckles on her face, but her eyes were friendly

and she seemed to know who they were even before they said a word.

"Follow me," she said as she walked by them and put down her load of plates next to the old man with soapsuds up to his elbows.

They followed her past counters piled high with dishes through a little door that led into a dark room. When they were all inside, the light snapped on and the door slammed shut. Peter looked around to see that they were standing in a small storeroom not much bigger than a large closet. The walls were lined with shelves, and the place smelled like disinfectant.

Elise broke the silence. "Who are you?"

The girl untied a white apron and hung it up on a nail next to the door. She found her brown leather jacket hanging from a collection of coats next to the door and put it on. Then she shook her red hair.

"My cousin Erik sent the note," she told them. "I'm Evy. He worked in the Resistance during the war, and now I'm helping him."

Peter wanted to ask what she was helping him with now, but he didn't dare. Instead Peter, Elise, and Henrik introduced themselves in turn.

"Erik heard you were looking for the people on the plane," said Evy after they had told her who they were.

"You know about it?" asked Henrik eagerly.

Evy nodded. "A little. People heard it come in low over the island yesterday around lunchtime. It landed at the airstrip outside town, and now the Russians have locked up the pilot."

"But Captain Ivanov said he didn't know anything about a plane," objected Peter.

"Captain Ivanov is lying." Evy handed them each a coat. "The Russians are supposed to be our friends, but no one trusts them. Of course, they don't trust anyone else, so that figures. They think everyone who comes to the island is a nuclear spy. They need to leave."

"So you know where my mother is?" asked Henrik.

Evy shook her head. "I'm not sure. But if your mother was on that plane, they're probably holding her in their headquarters, or maybe up at the airstrip. The last time this happened, the Russians just took the pilot off the island and no one ever heard anything about it."

"Why are you giving us these coats?" asked Elise. She was looking at the large gray overcoat Evy had handed her.

"You don't want to get cold, do you?"

Elise shook her head.

"All right. Our group wants to make sure the Russians leave the island as soon as possible. You help us, we help you. Erik is taking us out to the airport to see if we can find anything."

"Sounds good to me," agreed Henrik, pulling on his coat and heading for the door.

"Hold it." Evy grabbed Henrik's arm and nodded toward the back of the little room. "We're going out the other way."

Henrik and the twins looked curiously in the direction Evy pointed.

"One at a time," she continued, "through the Mission Hotel's deluxe elevator."

THE FIRST CLUE

Evy pulled open what looked like a cabinet door the size of a window, revealing a box just big enough to crawl into. A pair of heavy ropes ran up and down a shaft to the left of the box, something like the ones used to raise and lower a flag on a flagpole.

"Hey, it's a dumbwaiter!" said Henrik. "You mean we're going to . . ."

Evy grinned when she showed Peter and Elise the miniature freight elevator. "Sure, you're going to ride in it. We do it all the time. The Germans never figured out how we used to get out of the building. Now the Russians haven't figured it out, either. Peter, you go first. Get out in the basement and wait for us there."

Peter obeyed, crawling carefully into the doghouse-sized hand-elevator. The side of the box was open so that he could have controlled the ropes himself if he had been strong enough, but he just huddled and watched as he was lowered deeper into a dark shaft. A few seconds later, the tiny elevator bumped to a stop.

"You're at the bottom," hissed Evy from the storeroom above. "Get out and wait."

Peter took a breath and groped out into the darkness. His toes finally hit a solid floor, and he slipped out of the elevator.

"Okay, I'm out," he called back up the shaft. He heard the ropes and then the elevator was gone.

As his eyes got used to the darkness, he began to notice shapes in the room, then the faint light from a high window. A moment later the elevator arrived with a little thud.

"Are you there?" whispered Elise.

Peter reached out and took his sister by the arm. "Right here."

"It's so dark down here."

Once more the elevator disappeared, only to reappear once more with Henrik. Peter and Elise pulled him out and waited for their red-haired guide.

"All right," announced Evy when she had lowered herself to where they stood waiting. "You kids follow me." She slipped a flashlight out of her pocket and pointed the dull light ahead.

"What about our uncle?" Elise worried aloud. "We need to tell him where we're going. He's not going to know where we are."

"Don't worry," Evy assured them as she led them through the basement. "Erik took care of that. Besides, we'll be back in just a few minutes."

She checked the back alley carefully, then slipped outside.

"I guess that means we have to follow her," said Peter, slipping out the door and climbing a few steps to the alley.

Outside it seemed even darker than before, and what used to be a house in back of the hotel was completely in ruins. Peter shivered, then turned back to the stairwell to help Elise up to the street as a pair of headlights caught them like a flash photo. When the car stopped right next to them, Peter didn't know whether to run or jump back into the basement.

"It's Erik," reported Evy. "Let's go."

The car was large and ancient with an unlit "TAXI" sign bolted to the top. When the door creaked open, Peter could see a teenager in a heavy coat sitting in the worn leather driver's seat, with a red elf's hat on his head.

"Come on," said the elf. "You're slow, Evy."

"Sorry," she replied, slipping into the front seat. "I had to get them all down the elevator."

"All right," he replied. "I'm supposed to get this taxi back to Anders in half an hour, so we'd better hurry."

Peter noticed the teenage elf looking at them in the rearview mirror as they raced along the harbor road, past the dark shapes of several ships. He had bright, curious-looking eyes and a short button nose. And his dark hair was sticking out wildly from under the funny hat, which was pushed back on his head.

"So have you kids been nice this year?" asked the driver. "Don't answer that."

"Erik," Evy scolded the driver with a smile. "They haven't met you before."

"Oh, sorry." He poked his right hand back for someone to shake. "I'm the Christmas elf. Pleased to meet you."

Elise took her turn shaking the elf's hand. "I'm Elise, and this is my brother, Peter, and our friend Henrik."

"Christmasman here is really Erik Torp," explained Evy. "We're going to a Christmas party a little later. He also likes to be real mysterious, so I usually have to explain to people what he's doing."

"That's me," replied Erik, smiling back at them. "I thought if we were stopped on the way out to the airport, the Russians might get a kick out of the hat."

Peter thought of something. "Torp! So you're the one who's related to Ole and Gerta Torp, right?"

"Hey, you know my dad's cousin Ole?" answered the driver, swerving. "Or is it second cousin? I'm not sure. Anyway, it's a small world. How is he? I heard he was going to come to the island to help with the hotel, but then the bombing kind of changed things."

"Actually, we hardly know them," admitted Elise. "But they're fine. They stayed in Henrik's apartment while Henrik and his family were in Sweden. And now Ole just got a job in Hillerod. We saw them right before we got the phone call to come here."

"Is that right?" Erik seemed interested. "What phone call was that?"

Peter was confused. "You're not the one who called us in Helsingor?"

Erik glanced back at them once more through his mirror. "Call you? How would I do that when I had no idea who you were until just now?"

"Someone called us yesterday," explained Elise. "The voice sounded kind of like yours. Anyway, that's how we knew to come here with our Uncle Morten. A phone call."

"And the guy on the phone said we should get here as soon as we could," added Henrik, "because the Russians might not let my mom go. But he was acting like it was a big secret."

"Evy?" questioned Erik, turning in his seat. "Do you have any idea who it could have been?"

"Keep your eyes on the road, Erik," she replied. "It wasn't anyone we worked with. I have no idea."

"Hmm . . ." Erik shifted gears once more as they climbed a small hill, then pulled over to the side of the road and switched off his headlights as they glided to a stop in the gravel.

"Can you tell us what's going on?" asked Henrik.

The older boy turned around. "Okay, here's what I can tell you. We know that a small plane landed here yesterday. I don't know if it crash-landed or just landed, but it's here. We know it's not Russian, and a fellow who saw it coming down said it might have been red. But that's all the information we have."

"Where is it?" asked Peter.

"The airport is just over there." Erik pointed to the right of the car. "Just over the top of this little hill. There's usually a Russian guard or two, but my guess is they'll be inside tonight, out of the cold."

"And so what exactly are we looking for?" asked Peter.

"Your mom's plane, of course," replied Erik. "That's the first step to finding her."

"That's *my* mom," put in Henrik. "Not Peter and Elise's."

Erik pulled off his cap and pushed open his door. "Whatever. Let's go take a look."

"Right," said Henrik, pushing open his door.

"Wait a minute!" warned Erik. "We don't just go running out there. Evy, you and one of the kids go check out the hangars, see if you can find a plane. I'll take the other two, and we'll go see if we can find anything inside the airport building. Meet back here in ten minutes."

Peter hesitated, wondering how they would split up. But Evy tapped his arm before she slipped out the door.

"Come with me, Peter," she told him, and he nodded. Flicking on her flashlight, Evy led the way up a small dirt path, over the little hill, and back down to where the airport lay stretched out in the darkness. In front of them only a faint light shone from a building that looked like the office. One large, old German military plane sat in front of the building, sagging from neglect. A windsock to tell the direction of the wind flapped from a pole in front of the building in the cold breeze. The only other sound was someone laughing from far away.

"Come on," whispered Evy. "There's no one in the hangar."

While Erik headed toward the building with the light, Evy and Peter circled around to another, larger building with a rounded roof.

"This is where they keep all their planes," she told him. "Let's try the door."

Peter jiggled the ice-cold doorknob and looked over his shoulder nervously. "Locked."

"Of course it is. What about this window?"

Peter stood on his tiptoes to push on one small window high up, which wouldn't budge. On the other side, Evy pulled something shiny out of her pocket.

"What's that?" asked Peter.

"Screwdriver. Good for fixing locked windows."

"But you're going to break it!"

Evy sighed but didn't stop prying. A moment later there was

a popping sound as the latch turned and the window swung open into the dark airplane hangar.

"Erik taught me how to do this during the war," she explained.

"Well, sure," he began, "but . . ."

"Listen," she told him, "we're not burglars, and I wouldn't worry about hurting the Russians' feelings, if that's what you're thinking. We're just trying to find out about your mother."

Peter didn't try to correct her, only wondered what would happen if a Russian soldier happened to see them just then. Evy bent down with her hands together in front, like a stirrup for Peter to climb.

"Okay," she told him. "Up you go."

Peter did as he was told, climbing through the tiny window and tumbling over into the darkness inside.

"Watch out," whispered Evy before dropping lightly to the cold concrete floor beside him. "Here I come."

When she got to her feet, Evy switched on her flashlight again and pointed its weak yellow circle of light at the floor. Peter could make out a workbench littered with tools and greasy black things that looked like engine parts. In the distance, he saw the shadows of two or three warplanes inside the large, high-ceilinged hangar. Peter whistled softly and walked over to one of the shadows.

"Wow, look at this thing," he whispered.

"That's not the one," replied Evy, shining her light on the large, faded red star on the side of the plane, just below the tail. "I think some of their generals come in and out of Moscow on this kind—"

The sound of the door rattling made Evy freeze in midsentence. She snapped off her light and grabbed for Peter's arm. They stood still for a long minute, but there was no other sound until Evy whispered into Peter's ear, "Just a guard. We need to be careful when we leave."

Wishing he could feel as cool as Evy sounded, Peter tried to keep up with her in the dark. Somehow, he couldn't shake the feeling that the sleeping giants all around him would suddenly wake up if he made a sound. Then to the side, between two larger Russian planes, he thought he saw something different.

"Over here," he whispered while stepping carefully over to the smaller shape. Evy joined him and snapped her light on a small, private plane, different from the war planes all around them. It looked like a tiny two-seater, painted a bright red and looking quite out of place.

"Maybe this is it," he said, trying the small door underneath the wings. He bumped his head on the overhead wing.

"Ouch," said Peter. "Watch your head."

"This has to be it," agreed Evy. "See anything inside?"

The flashlight started to fade out, and Evy thumped it in the palm of her hand.

"Shine it on the front seat," said Peter, opening the door on the pilot's side. The little plane had two small seats in front, with a tiny storage area tucked in behind. It looked only big enough for a small suitcase, but he supposed someone could wedge themselves in behind the pilot's seat if they wanted to.

"Nothing here," Peter announced, feeling the seat as the light winked out once more. "Just a map and—wait a minute . . ."

His hand brushed against a strap of some sort, and he pulled out a purse from under the front seat.

With a last flicker from the flashlight, they looked inside the purse. A comb, a small green box of Swedish "Läkerol" licorice throat lozenges, an old black book with a few envelopes stuffed inside the pages, and a leather wallet with an identification card. Ruth Melchior's identification card!

Peter snapped the little black leather handbag shut. "This is it. This is Henrik's mother's!"

"Good boy! That's what we needed. I'm just surprised the Russians didn't find it before us. Now let's get out of here. The others are probably waiting by now."

Peter turned eagerly and retraced his steps back to the door, when something occurred to him.

The book in the purse! The one they were looking for!

He stopped short and opened up the purse once more, digging around for the book. But it was too dark, and everything spilled out on the cement floor.

"What are you doing?" whispered Evy. "I think someone's coming again."

Peter panicked and dropped to his knees in the darkness but said nothing. He found the wallet and the comb, but the throat lozenges were gone.

"Where's that book?" he asked himself desperately.

"Shh!" warned Evy. They listened once more but heard nothing, so Evy found her way back to the window, leaving Peter groping on the floor. He found a screwdriver, then a wadded-up piece of paper that felt like a gum wrapper, but no book.

It couldn't have flown away!

Evy snapped her fingers quietly at the window, waiting for Peter to catch up. He swept his fingers across the cement once more, trying to force his eyes to see into the shadows.

"Come on, Peter! We have to go!"

Just then Peter's fingers closed on the rough cover of the book, which had landed several steps behind him. It was closed, and he could feel the envelopes still tucked inside. Peter heaved a sigh of relief, stuffed the book into the purse, and jumped up to follow Evy.

At the window Evy turned around and made a stirrup once more with her hands. Peter stepped up, but his shoulder brushed against something on the wall. Suddenly, he was looking at Evy in the bright glare of an overhead light.

Peter felt like a deer trapped in front of a car's headlights, unable to move. But Evy reached over with a quick move of her hand and flipped the lights back off.

"Hurry!" she told him, her voice cracking. "Watch out for guards and run for the car. We may have just announced to the entire Russian army that we're out here."

Peter clutched the purse more tightly and bit his lip. *How could I have been so clumsy?*

But a moment later he was back outside the hangar, crouching in the darkness. In the distance the lights were still on in the airport office. He saw the dark shape of someone standing behind a parked car in front of the office, looking in their direction, but the person ducked before Peter could tell who it was. At the same time, someone else grabbed him by the shoulder, and Peter's heart jumped.

"It's just me," whispered the dark figure. "Erik. Where's Evy? And what's with all the lights?"

Peter caught his breath and stood up as the window above him squeaked. "She's coming. It was an accident. But if *you're* here, who's over there by that car?"

Evy dropped quietly to the ground beside them and pulled the window back into place.

"Find anything?" asked Erik. "What took you so long?"

"Tell you back at the car," whispered Evy, brushing past them. Peter looked around for his sister and Henrik.

"Wait a minute," he said. "Where are the others?"

"They're waiting back at the taxi," replied Erik. "Come on."

Peter looked over at the airport office again, at the car where he had seen the other shadow, but there was no one. Maybe he had just been seeing things, he told himself. Glad to get away, he followed Erik and Evy as they stumbled back over the low hill between the car and the edge of the airport. Peter ran faster when he saw the dark shape of the taxi, and the back door swung open when he stepped up.

"We were starting to wonder," said Elise when Peter slipped into the bench seat beside her. He slammed and locked the door before he answered while Erik tried to start the car.

"Uh-oh," he murmured.

"What's the matter?" asked Henrik.

The car made a clicking sound but didn't start.

"Uh, it's an old car," admitted Erik. "Everybody back out. We have to push."

Everyone piled out and took positions behind the car while Erik waved at them from the driver's seat. "Go ahead and push, and when I wave my hand, step away. GO!"

Together they pushed harder and harder, bringing the old

black car up to speed. Finally Erik waved his hand and shouted out the window, "Let me go!"

The car coasted silently for a few yards, then jerked as Erik put it in gear. The engine sputtered, then roared to life.

They all ran to catch up and piled back into the waiting taxi.

"Thanks!" said Erik as the twins and Henrik caught their breath in the backseat. "It's a little easier to start with a good pushing crew like you."

Peter nodded. "Uh-huh."

"So what's the report?" asked Erik, making a U-turn in the middle of the dark road and steering back in the direction of town. "All we saw were ten Russian soldiers sitting around, having their usual party."

"Christmas party?" asked Peter.

Erik shook his head. "I don't think so. The Russians celebrate their Christmas a few days later than we do. Anyway, we couldn't see any prisoners or any place they could have been holding a prisoner."

"Well, at least we found their plane," announced Evy.

"Really?" asked Henrik, leaning over the front seat. "Are you sure?"

Peter pulled the purse out from under his coat. "We're sure. We found this under the seat, Henrik. It has your mom's wallet inside and everything."

Erik turned his head. "That's great. Now we know for sure the Russians have your mother somewhere. All we have to do is find her."

Henrik leaned back in his seat, the purse in his lap, and said nothing as they continued on.

"Well," continued their driver, "that's about as much as we can do tonight. We're going to drop you off back at the hotel. I hope your uncle isn't too worried."

"I thought Evy said you took care of telling him," said Elise.

"I couldn't. Old Captain Ivanov had him cornered in the dining room with a couple of other officers, and it looked like they were giving him a pretty tough interview. I couldn't get close to tell him anything."

Peter groaned. "Oh, great. We're in trouble now."

Erik stopped the car in the alley behind the hotel, the same place he had picked them up. "No, listen. You've only been gone for half an hour. Just go back into the hotel the same way Evy took you out. You'll be fine."

"Just half an hour?" Peter wondered aloud. It had seemed at least twice that.

"We'll find you tomorrow," promised Evy. "And then we'll see what we can do about finding your mom. *Glaedelig Jul!* Merry Christmas!"

"Thanks," said Elise, taking the older girl's hand.

"Yeah, thanks," echoed Henrik.

The three of them climbed out into the alley and stood shivering as the car disappeared. Somewhere a piano was playing "Silent Night."

"Let's get back inside," said Elise, leading the way down the stairs to the basement door where they had come out. Peter tried to follow but bumped into Henrik from behind.

"It's locked," groaned Elise.

"Here, let me try," said Henrik, stepping up to the door. But he could only shake the door on its hinges, the way Elise had.

"It won't budge," he admitted. "Somebody's locked it."

"Well, we could always go back in through the front door, the way we did the first time," suggested Peter.

No one said anything, so they all tiptoed around the building to the front entry. Soldiers were coming and going, laughing and singing strange Russian songs.

"Why are we still tiptoeing?" asked Elise. "Let's just slip in behind these guys and sit in the lobby for a while."

The soldiers ignored them as they stepped into the lobby and hung up their coats. A large Christmas tree next to the front desk was decked out with strings of bright red-and-white Danish flags and bits of tinsel, just like their tree at home.

"I hadn't noticed this here before," Peter said to himself. Elise and Henrik joined him, and they found a place to sit down—behind the Christmas tree in some stiff wooden chairs set up along the wall of the small, bare lobby. There was no one at the hotel's front desk.

"Now what?" asked Henrik, blowing on his hands to warm them up.

Peter's cheeks were burning from the cold. Then he remembered. "Oh yeah, check out the purse, Henrik," he said, sitting down next to his friend. "There's something else inside."

"Right here?" Henrik opened the purse carefully, as if it would explode.

"The book we were looking for—it's there," said Peter. "The envelopes, too. Matthias must have given them to your mom."

Henrik pulled out the slender black book Peter had dropped in the airplane hangar. In the light, it looked even older than Peter had thought, and the cover was cracked and weathered. Gold lettering on what would have been the back cover was faded and barely readable, but it was obviously not Danish.

"It really *is* a Hebrew book," whispered Henrik, turning it over carefully in his hands. He opened it and turned a couple of the yellowed, brittle pages. Inside, Peter could see the strange lines and shapes that made Hebrew writing so different from the letters they were used to. Many of the sentences had been underlined and a few words were circled—perhaps the work of a scholar who had read the words and understood them. But as different as it was, something seemed familiar about the writing.

"So that's the book we've been looking for?" asked Elise.

Henrik nodded. "Looks like it belonged to my grandfather." He pointed to a faded signature on the back flap.

"Jonas Melchior." Peter read the fine, careful script.

"Too bad we can't read Hebrew," said Elise, taking a look herself. "Could your father?"

Henrik shook his head. "Not really. He knew a little, but I think my grandfather Jonas was the last one in my family who could really read it. I never knew him."

For a moment Peter thought back to the last night of Hanukkah, when Matthias Karlsson had visited the Melchiors. He remembered the candles they had lit and the Hebrew prayers. Of course!

"Hey, Henrik, I know somebody who can read your book."

"I know." Henrik's eyes lit up like a red traffic light. "Don't say it."

"But what about the envelopes?" asked Elise.

"I was just getting to that." Henrik's hands were shaking as he pulled out two small envelopes from between the pages of the book. On the outside of the first one, someone had written a woman's name.

"Esther," read Elise. "It's in the same handwriting. Was that your grandmother?"

Henrik nodded. "She died before I was born, like my grandfather."

He opened the flap of the envelope, paused, and sighed.

"So what's inside, Henrik?" Elise leaned over to see, and Henrik held up the empty envelope. He put his fingers inside, wiggled them around, and passed the envelope to her.

"That's it?" asked Peter. "A dried-up rose? What about the other one?"

Henrik showed them the other envelope, empty as well. Then he turned the old book upside down and leafed through the pages, shaking it gently.

"That's the big mystery message we've been looking for," he said, closing the book with a frown on his face. "And the message is that there is no message."

Peter wrinkled his eyebrows and studied the empty envelopes again. "Can't be. Maybe your mom has the real message."

"No," Henrik disagreed. "That's it. My dad said it was important, but he must have been thinking of something else. I don't know. I guess I'll never know."

"But we just can't give up like that," insisted Elise.

"You have any better ideas?" Henrik slumped down in his chair.

"Well," suggested Peter. "We still have to find your mom."

"Yeah." Henrik nodded. "We still do."

"There you are!" boomed Uncle Morten, hurrying toward them from the restaurant. His face looked drained and worried, but he forced a smile. "I am so sorry."

"Sorry for what?" asked Elise, getting to her feet.

"Well, for keeping you kids waiting all this time. That Riznik fellow didn't stay around, and the other translator they gave us could hardly speak Danish."

"So what did you do?" Elise wanted to know.

"Well, those Russian fellows just wouldn't let me go, asked me the same questions over and over. I think they finally decided I wasn't going to tell them anything after all, and they wanted to get back to their party."

"We've been fine," said Peter, looking around the room. Another group of loud soldiers came storming through the front door with a rush of cold air. "But we need to tell you something."

Entertaining Angels

"Tell you what," replied Uncle Morten. "How about if you save it for when we get settled here. I did find out that this hotel is completely full tonight. But the fellow at the front desk said he would call his father, who owns the biggest fishing boat on the island. It's out in the harbor—I think near where we docked the *Anna Marie*."

"You mean we're going to sleep on a fishing boat tonight?" asked Elise.

Their uncle nodded. "Looks like it. Get your coats, and I'll make sure it's still all right. Oh, and I'd better try to call Lisbeth at home."

Elise hurried into the dining room where they had left their coats while Peter and Henrik waited in the lobby for Uncle Morten. They waited for another ten minutes, pacing the lobby and trying to stay out of the way of the Russians.

"I was thinking we might have to sleep on the *Anna Marie*," said Henrik, looking up at the lobby clock once more.

Peter laughed. "That would have been something. You and I could sleep on the engine, while Elise gets the only bunk. And out in the cold."

"That would leave just about enough room for me to sleep standing up next to the steering wheel with the cat," added Uncle Morten, returning from a back room with a covered plate.

"The cat!" said Peter. "Do you think Tiger is still okay?"

"I'm sure he's fine," answered Uncle Morten, pulling the paper off the plate he was carrying to show a pile of meat scraps. "But maybe he's hungry."

"Where did you get that, Uncle Morten?" asked Peter, taking the plate.

"Kitchen scraps."

"Did you get through to Lisbeth?" asked Elise.

Uncle Morten nodded as he held the front door for them. "She's fine. They haven't heard anything else. But if they do, they know where to call now."

When everyone had their coats on, the four of them left the hotel together and retraced their steps, the way they had come through the streets from the harbor. Peter hurried on ahead with the cat food.

"I'll feed Tiger and get our bags," Peter volunteered when they reached the *Anna Marie*. Henrik followed him as they stepped on board the little boat.

"Tiger?" Henrik found a flashlight from a shelf and snapped it on. The wheelhouse was just as they had left it hours before.

"Tii-ger!" Peter whistled. "Come and get some dinner, boy."

Peter put down the plate and whistled again, the same way he did at home. Usually that would bring the cat at a run.

"He's not here," said Henrik, shining the light into the sleeping nook, where Tiger had stowed away before. There was no sign of the cat. Peter even lifted up a floorboard to check down underneath in the engine compartment. Still no Tiger.

"Find him?" Uncle Morten leaned across from the dock and poked his head into the wheelhouse.

"He's not here, Uncle Morten," answered Peter, taking a deep breath. "The soldiers must have scared him off, and now he's lost."

"Put the food down on the deck of the boat," replied their uncle. "He'll be back."

It was all Peter could do. While Henrik collected their three overnight bags from inside the cabin, Peter found a place on the forward deck for the plate.

"Come on back, Tiger," he whispered into the darkness. "You don't want to get lost here."

Finally he turned and jumped off the boat to follow Henrik, who had gone on ahead with their bags. Uncle Morten put his hand on Peter's shoulder.

"He can take care of himself," said Uncle Morten. "Remember how you found him? He was a lost alley cat once before, remember."

Peter nodded and looked into the shadows around the pier where Henrik flashed their light. He remembered how the cat had found him in the Copenhagen office building where the Nazis had once held him and Elise, Uncle Morten, and Lisbeth prisoner.

"I remember," said Peter. "But he was only a kitten."

"Still, he'll be fine." Uncle Morten took the flashlight as they continued toward the end of the pier. "And right now we'd better find our hotel. The man said it was the biggest boat around. Look for one called the *Cecilie*."

They didn't have far to look. The biggest boat in the harbor was lit up like a Christmas tree, with lanterns in the wheelhouse window and smoke rising from a small smokestack. Peter looked down the line of fishing boats to compare; this one was at least three times as long as their *Anna Marie*, tied up only a few boats away. A side door by the main wheelhouse opened as they approached, and an old man's voice boomed out.

"You're the Andersens? Don't just stand there looking. Come get in out of the cold, for goodness' sake!"

Peter was glad to obey the friendly voice. They slipped over the railing and followed their uncle into the wheelhouse.

Inside it was toasty warm, even compared to the hotel, but at first there was no one to be seen.

"Where did he go?" wondered Elise.

"Down here," called the voice, and they followed Uncle Morten down a small ladder-stairway to a galley and eating area. Lit by the cheery glow of four kerosene lanterns hung on the wall, Peter could see a large, polished wooden eating table, ringed by comfortable-looking dark green cushioned benches. In the far corner, a small wood stove popped and hissed, sending welcome waves of warm air throughout the room.

Behind the table, a small man dressed in a baggy red sweater was hunched over a cook stove. He looked too old to have moved so quickly from upstairs, but he smiled broadly as he turned around with a steaming teakettle in his grip. Peter took one look at the little gnome of a man and decided that they had discovered the original Christmasman.

"Welcome to the *Cecilie,*" said the little man. He was bent over and wrinkled, but he moved quickly to pour steaming water out into four waiting mugs on the table. His silvery white beard bobbed when he spoke, and the friendly man laughed as they stared.

"And Merry Christmas, by the way. It's not often we get visitors on Christmas Eve. I apologize for the hotel being so full. My grandchildren told me."

Uncle Morten began to loosen his coat. "Grandchildren?"

"Erik and Evy. Didn't you meet them at the hotel where they work? My son works there, too."

"We met them," said Peter, shaking the man's hand. It felt kind of like a tree root, twisted and rough. And Peter noticed that he held them more like hooks than real hands. But the man's eyes twinkled with life in the warm yellow lamplight.

"I'm Peter."

"Torp," said the old man as he took everyone's hand. "Uffe Torp."

"Looks like everyone is related here on this island," said Uncle Morten.

"One way or another," agreed the man with a smile.

It took Peter a few seconds to figure out the connections. Erik's dad, who was Evy's uncle, worked at the hotel. They hadn't met him. And this man, Uffe Torp, was their grandfather, who was also related . . .

"And there were the Torps back in Hillerod," added Peter.

Henrik chuckled. "We're sure lucky to run into all you people."

The jolly old man put his head back and laughed. "Luck? No such thing."

Peter had a feeling he knew what the man meant, and Elise gave him a smile of understanding, too. But he wasn't sure from Henrik's puzzled expression that his friend quite knew what the elder Mr. Torp was hinting at.

"And it's awfully nice of you to let us use your—" began Elise.

"It's nothing," interrupted the old man, sitting them down with steaming mugs of tea. "We couldn't have you sleeping on the street for Christmas like the Little Match Girl."

Peter took off his coat and laid it on a bench before he sat down with the others. Like every other Danish young person, he remembered the Hans Christian Andersen fairy tale about the homeless girl trying to sell matches on the street and keep warm on Christmas Eve.

"And besides," continued the man, "my grandson Erik reminded me that you might be angels."

"Angels?" Uncle Morten laughed. "You wouldn't say that if you knew these kids. They have a funny way of finding trouble."

The old man smiled and pointed to Peter's bag, then looked at Henrik. "Tell you what, young man. Looks like your Bible is about to fall out of that hole in your bag. Seeing that it's Christmas, you won't mind reading something out of it before I go. Pull it out here, would you please?"

Henrik began to open his mouth but did as he was told. There seemed no way to say no to the man with the white beard.

"Thirteenth chapter of Hebrews. I'd read it for you myself, but my eyes aren't as good as they used to be."

Henrik opened Peter's little black New Testament and leafed

through a few pages with a lost expression while Elise leaned over to help him.

"First Timothy, Second Timothy," she whispered, "then Titus, Philemon, then the Letter to the Hebrews."

"Letter to the Hebrews," repeated Henrik. "A letter to Jewish people?"

Elise nodded, and Henrik cleared his throat shyly, looking for the right verse. He glanced up at Peter, then put his finger back down to find his place.

"Um, it says, 'Do not forget to entertain strangers, for by so doing some people have entertained angels without knowing it.' Is that the verse?"

Old Mr. Torp smiled. "That's the one. Probably talking about Abraham entertaining angels in the Old Testament, but I suppose you never know. You're sure you're not angels?"

This time everyone laughed, except Henrik, who was still reading the Bible to himself. His forehead was wrinkled in thought, and Peter looked over his shoulder to see Henrik's finger fixed on the verse following the one he had just read out loud.

"Remember those in prison as if you were their fellow prisoners," Peter read silently, *"and those who are mistreated as if you yourselves were suffering."*

"So what did you find out at the airport?" Mr. Torp finally asked. Henrik looked up from his reading in surprise.

"Airport?" asked Uncle Morten. "Is there something I should know here?"

"That's what we were trying to tell you back at the hotel, Uncle Morten," said Elise. "Erik and Evy . . ."

Elise, Peter, and Henrik took turns explaining what they had discovered at the airport. Henrik saved the part about his mother's purse for last, pulling it out of his big coat pocket and showing it around.

"Well, now we know for certain that your mother is here somewhere," Uncle Morten told Henrik. "I just wish you kids had talked to me first, before you went sneaking around."

"If I know my grandchildren," said old Mr. Torp, looking at

the twins, "it was their idea, right?"

Peter and Elise nodded.

"Evy was real nice," said Elise. "And I think Erik tried to tell you where we were going, Uncle Morten. But the Russians . . ."

"I know, I know." Uncle Morten shook his head. "The Russians had my full attention for a while. From now on, let's try to stay together as much as we can, all right?"

Henrik and the twins nodded seriously.

"Well, I know we're not angels," answered Uncle Morten. "But I'm not so sure about you, Mr. Torp, helping us out the way you have. And we certainly appreciate it, especially at Christmas. You should be back with your family, celebrating."

The old man held up his hand and nodded, and again Peter had to keep from staring. *If anyone is Christmasman, this is him*, he thought.

"I'll get back soon enough," Mr. Torp told them. "Or at least as soon as these eighty-four-year-old man's legs can carry me. It's just a shame you won't join us."

"Oh no." Uncle Morten shook his head. "I told your son at the hotel already that we're enough trouble as it is."

"Well then, we'll see you in the morning. Put some more coal in the stove when you get cold, and there are some bunks made up." He motioned to a doorway and a wood-paneled hall with several more rooms.

"Thank you again," said Uncle Morten, helping the old man with his coat. Mr. Torp stopped and turned toward the kids.

"We're going to find your mother, young fellow," he told Henrik with a gentle smile. "The whole church is praying for you. And we'll see you in the morning. Merry Christmas."

Peter almost heard Henrik swallow hard.

"Uh, thanks," said Henrik, looking uncertainly back at Mr. Torp as he left them alone in the boat. "Merry Christmas."

Elise waited for Mr. Torp to disappear up the ladder before she cleared her throat. "Are you sure you guys don't believe in Christmasman anymore?"

"You know I never did when I was little," said Henrik, getting up from the table. "But now I'm not so sure."

"I'm sure," offered Peter, almost half seriously. "That was him. The beard. The elf look. Everything except the red suit. Now the only thing that's missing is a little Christmas tree here on the ship."

The twins and Henrik explored the rest of their floating hotel, which was larger inside than it had looked to Peter even from the outside. The hallway that stretched toward the back end of the ship from the eating area had three compact rooms on each side. On the left, each one had a built-in bunk bed and a small closet space to hang clothes. On the right was first a navigation room with a slanted table for charts. Next was a small bathroom, and finally a larger room with a single bed covered in a plaid wool blanket.

"This must be the captain's bedroom," said Elise, peeking inside and trying the mattress with her hand. "He's got the nicest bed."

"Yeah, and the bunk beds are pretty neat, too," said Peter, crawling over the bed to the porthole window. "But we'd better close this porthole. All the cold air is coming in."

Peter paused for a minute to peek out the tiny window, then he whistled softly. "Tiger! Are you out there?"

Something moved, but Peter knew right away it wasn't the cat. The two Russian guards in their fur caps, the same ones who had first met them when they arrived in the *Anna Marie*, were standing watch not twenty feet away. One of them was rubbing his gloved hands together to keep warm; the other was staring straight at them.

Night Visitor

"Mr. Torp says not to worry about the guards out on the pier," said Uncle Morten when he came back down the stairs. "He says they're keeping an eye on us, but they're no threat."

"No threat," repeated Henrik, looking out one of the portholes by the galley sink. "So why don't they just go back to their Christmas party and leave us alone?"

Uncle Morten shrugged and smiled. "Just pull the curtains and try not to worry."

Peter looked at the porthole. "We would, Uncle Morten, if there were any curtains."

Elise giggled and retreated down the hallway with her bag. "Well, boys, I don't know about you, but I think I'll go to bed. Christmasman has already been here for the night."

"He said he was coming back in the morning, right?" asked Henrik.

Peter nodded as he picked up his own bag. "We'll find your mom, Henrik. She's here. Matthias too. The Russians will figure out they're not spies."

"Matthias." Henrik repeated the name as if for the first time.

Then he turned to find his bunk. Peter noticed that his pocket
Bible was still in Henrik's back pocket.

"Good night, Henrik," Peter called after his friend. He decided
not to say anything about the Bible.

"See you in the morning, Peter."

Peter tried to fall asleep in his compact little bunk, but he just
tossed and turned. He wondered if they would really find Henrik's mom, the way he had told Henrik. Outside, he knew, the
Russians were still watching them.

It has to be pretty cold and boring out there, he thought, and his
thoughts turned into a prayer.

*Lord, please help us find Henrik's mom before the Russians take her
away to Moscow, or wherever they take spies. Even though she's not a
spy.*

Before he fell asleep, his thoughts drifted back to the events
of the past month—their search for Henrik's missing book, the
mysterious phone call, and everyone they had met since then. He
wasn't sure how it all fit together, but he was sure this didn't feel
anything like a real Christmas.

And, Lord, Peter added, *please help us find Matthias . . . and Tiger,
too.* The musical sound of gentle waves slapping against the outside of the boat's wooden hull put him to sleep, but not for long.

How long have I been asleep? Peter wondered, drowsy but awake
again. In the next room, he could hear Henrik's bed squeaking,
and there was a dim light coming from the hallway. Quietly, he
slipped out of his bed and peeked around the corner into Henrik's
room.

Henrik was curled up in his bed, the covers pulled around his
shoulders. He was holding a flashlight on his shoulder, the weak
yellow beam barely lighting up the pages of a little book. Peter's
Bible.

Peter smiled to himself and wondered what part Henrik was
reading. Maybe the book of Hebrews, the part old Mr. Torp had
asked Henrik to read. Peter almost laughed to himself, remem-

bering how the old man had thought the Bible belonged to Henrik. Silently, Peter backed up and slipped into his bunk.

———————

When Peter woke the next time, it was still dark, still quiet. And he wondered if maybe Henrik was still reading next door. He had the sure impression that something, or someone, had awakened him.

"Henrik?" he whispered into the darkness. "Are you awake?" He wasn't sure just yet which direction Henrik's bunk was. In fact, in the darkness, he had to think for a minute where he was exactly. Then he heard the noise again—the sound of someone coming down the ladder from the wheelhouse.

"Uncle Morten?" he asked the darkness, and the sound stopped. He thought about pulling the covers over his head and yelling, but instead he swung out of his bunk and slipped to the doorway of his tiny room. He would crawl down the hallway to his uncle's room and wake him up.

But maybe it was only his uncle out for a breath of air. The kitchen where they had been sitting before was full of dark shapes and eerie shadows. Peter shivered and tried to turn away, but out of the corner of his eye, he saw something move. And he knew it was not Uncle Morten.

The shadow lunged toward him, and Peter turned to run, but he couldn't seem to make his legs move quickly enough. In a single leap, the shadow grabbed Peter around the shoulders and held him against the wall. Peter tried to scream, but a hand clamped tightly against his mouth.

"Hey, don't scream," hissed the shadow. "I'm not going to hurt you."

Peter tried to struggle, but he couldn't move. The shadow held him in place.

Why doesn't someone else wake up? he wondered desperately, kicking the wall with his bare feet.

"Peter?" came the sleepy voice of his sister in the next room. "Peter, what's going on?"

"Listen, boy," came the shadow's voice again, and this time Peter recognized the same strange accent he had heard once before. But where had he heard it? In the hotel? On the phone?

Of course! Peter realized in an instant who had grabbed him. The voice on the phone, the one who had called them back home in Helsingor. Captain Ivanov's translator, Lieutenant Riznik! Why hadn't he recognized the voice before?

"Will you stop kicking?" asked the man quietly. "I have something to tell you."

"Peter?" Elise's voice trembled while Peter ordered his body to stop shaking and tried to nod. The man loosened his grip and dropped his hand from covering Peter's mouth.

"It's okay, Elise," croaked Peter. "I think it's the same guy who called us on the phone."

Peter saw the shadow shrink back, as if he had just been hit. Peter took a deep breath.

"Why are you here?" Peter asked the shadow, sounding braver than he felt.

"All right," said the man. "Just listen to what I tell you. Your mother is being taken to a place they call the Castle this morning sometime. She's with the Swede, Karlsson, and I heard they're both going to be taken to Moscow tomorrow and tried as spies."

"But they're not spies!" insisted Elise. "How could anyone think so?"

"I know that, but Moscow is not so trusting," answered the shadow. "You must promise not to tell anyone I've been here. Otherwise, I shall have to deny every word of it. Do I have your word?"

There was a long pause. "We won't say anything," whispered Peter.

"Except to our uncle," added Elise, and Peter nodded in the darkness.

Apparently satisfied, the shadow turned to go, then stopped.

"One more thing."

The shadow hesitated, then held up something and laid it on the table.

"I found this over at the airport. Is your name Esaias Melchior?"

Peter caught his breath at the question. "No, that's Henrik's dad."

"Well, this belongs to him."

The man turned once more and hurried back up the stairway the way he had come, and for a moment a light from somewhere outside outlined his face.

It's him! thought Peter. *Lieutenant Riznik is the one who was watching us when we came out of the hangar at the airport. And the envelope has to be one that fell out of Henrik's book.*

Still shivering in the cold dampness of the boat, Peter backed into his room to get dressed.

"What's going on out there?" Peter finally heard his uncle rumble from the other room. Then he heard Elise's voice, probably explaining what had just happened. Peter went to his tiny porthole but saw nothing on the dark pier. No soldiers, no shadows. In the next room, where Henrik had been sleeping, he heard a bell ringing, then a thump as someone fell to the wood floor.

Prisoners at the Castle

"Are you okay in there?" asked Peter as he slipped over to see what had happened to his friend.

There was a groaning sound coming from the floor, and finally Uncle Morten came with a copper ship's lantern in hand. Henrik was sprawled on the floor in his pajamas, rubbing his head. Peter's Bible had fallen on top of him, as if Henrik had fallen asleep reading. The ringing sound had stopped.

"I must have rolled out trying to get my alarm clock," he mumbled. Then he looked up at everyone staring into his little room and got to his feet. He looked down at the Bible and scooted it under the bunk with his bare foot. "I'm fine. The bed is just a little tippy, that's all."

"Well, Henrik," said Uncle Morten. "Maybe you should have set your alarm for just a few minutes earlier."

"Earlier?" Henrik looked confused as he pulled his coat on. Peter could see his breath in the bright yellow flicker of the lamp. "I set it for six-thirty as it is."

"Seems you and I already missed all the action this morning," said Uncle Morten. "Elise tells me we've had a visitor."

Peter and Elise had to retell their story for Henrik, who went to the window just as Peter had done.

"I don't see anyone out there anymore," he whispered back.

"Why are we whispering?" asked Elise.

"I don't know," said Uncle Morten, "but I'm going to get the stove going, and then we're going to need something to eat."

Peter's stomach grumbled in agreement at the mention of food.

"Oh, but, Henrik," he said. "The guy left an envelope for you on the table. He asked if I was Esaias Melchior."

"What was he, a postman?" Henrik grabbed the envelope and studied it in the soft yellow lamplight.

"Open it," urged Elise.

"Where did he get this?" asked Henrik, still studying the writing.

"From the airport, he said." Peter shivered once more. "Probably by the airplane. I think it must have fallen out of your dad's book."

Henrik still turned the envelope over and over, not opening it. "And he brought it here? Why would he do that?"

Elise leaned over to look at Henrik's letter. "Aren't you going to open it?"

The envelope wasn't sealed, so Henrik finally removed a folded, brittle-looking piece of paper.

"What does it say?" asked Peter.

Henrik's lips moved as he read, but he made no sound. Peter and Elise just watched him while Uncle Morten started a small blaze in the ship's tiny cast-iron stove. Henrik wrinkled his eyebrows as if he didn't understand everything, then shook his head slowly. Finally he handed the letter over to Peter.

"You can read it," Henrik told him quietly. "I'm not sure I understand it all, but you can read it."

"You mean you don't know why your dad thought it was so important?" Peter wondered.

Henrik shrugged. "Go ahead and read it. It's from twenty years ago. You tell me what it all means."

Peter looked down at the fine, careful script of the old letter, dated 1925. It looked just like the handwriting they had seen on the other envelope. The paper had been folded and refolded, faded as if from being read and reread.

" 'Dear Esaias,' " Peter began in a quiet voice. Elise and Uncle Morten listened carefully while Henrik stared out a porthole.

" 'Dear Esaias,' " Peter began again. " 'It's very hard to admit when you've been so wrong for so long. . . .' "

Peter looked up, realizing he was about to uncover a very personal message. But Henrik just stared out the window and made a little waving motion for him to continue.

" 'As a Jew, I've lived my whole life not knowing the Messiah. My father and his father before him told us to wait and watch. As your father, I've told you the same thing.' "

Peter looked up. "So this was from your grandfather to your dad?"

Again Henrik nodded. "Yeah. Go ahead."

Finding his place, Peter continued reading. " 'I've told you the same thing, but last year I read a book by an American rabbi. He had a lot to say about Palestine and how the people of God were returning to Jerusalem. It's very exciting.' " Peter took a deep breath. "You really want me to keep reading, Henrik?"

No one said anything for a long minute, while the waves in the harbor made tinkling sounds under the boat.

I guess that means yes, thought Peter.

" 'But even more exciting was how he showed that our Messiah had already come. He introduced me to the Messiah, the one he calls Yeshua. Jesus.' " Peter's voice trembled a little when he came to the next part. " 'Please don't wait, as I have. I want to show you now how the Scriptures come true in Yeshua. Then you can introduce my grandchildren to him someday, as well. Your loving father, Jonas.' "

Henrik wiped his cheek with his sleeve while Peter came up beside him and slipped the letter into Henrik's hand.

"Here," Peter told him quietly. "You'd better keep this."

Henrik just nodded and looked down at the letter, reading it again quietly. "Dad said a couple of times before he died that he wanted to talk to me."

"About this?" Uncle Morten asked gently.

Henrik shrugged. "I don't know. But there were always nurses and people around. Then we thought he was going to get better. I guess he never got a chance."

"I think he just did, in a way," said Uncle Morten, putting his hand on Henrik's shoulder.

Henrik was about to say something else, then he stiffened. "Wait a minute," he whispered, pulling back from the window. "Someone else is coming!"

"What do you mean?" asked Peter, moving to take a look.

Peter saw no one in the gray darkness, but they all heard a knock on the side of the fishing boat and felt a slight rocking motion as someone climbed aboard.

"Hallo," called a voice from up in the wheelhouse. "Everyone awake down here? It's getting late."

"It's Erik," said Elise, retreating to her room with her hands on her hair. "And I look like I just woke up."

"Maybe that's because you just woke up," said Peter. He looked out to see their new friend coming down the stairway, balancing a bulging paper sack in his arms.

"Thought I'd check to see how you were doing," said Erik. "My dad gave me a little snack from the hotel to bring you."

Erik pulled out apples, a loaf of French bread, and some rolls from the bag, along with a bottle of milk and a wheel of cheese covered in red wax. Henrik replaced the letter carefully in the envelope and tried to hold back a big yawn.

"Oh, so you got a good night's sleep?" Erik asked Henrik.

Henrik rubbed the sleep out of his half-open eyes and nodded. "Great," he answered, then yawned once more. "I just, uh, well, maybe I just didn't get quite enough sleep."

"Me neither," agreed Peter.

"Breakfast!" said Uncle Morten, smiling at Erik and rubbing his hands together. "Tell your father thank you."

Henrik chose an apple for himself. "Hmm. Yeah, thanks."

Even Elise finally came back out, her hair combed neatly and pulled back from her face.

"Erik," asked Peter between mouthfuls of cheese and bread, "can you tell us how to get to the Castle?"

The teenager gave him a curious look. "I could, but I don't think you'll get very close. It's right next to a Russian building. Why would you want to go there, anyway?"

Henrik tried one of the rolls. "My mother is supposed to be there."

Erik stopped chewing. "How do you know that?"

"We had a visitor," said Uncle Morten. "Not long before you came. Henrik and I slept through it."

"Who?" demanded the teenager.

Peter hesitated, remembering his promise to the man. Erik was helping them, but still . . .

Erik looked from Peter to Elise while Uncle Morten spoke up for them. "I'm sure it was too dark for the twins to see who it was for certain," he told them. "And they don't know anyone here."

"But you knew who it was, didn't you?" pressed Erik. Peter looked down, wondering what he could say. Outside their windows, a seagull screamed a morning greeting.

"He made us promise not to tell anyone," started Elise.

"Who made you promise?"

"That's what I mean," said Elise. "The Russian man who came into the boat told us that Henrik's mom was in the building next to the Castle, and then he left."

"All right. A Russian. But did he say anything else?"

Peter cut himself another piece of bread. "He said they were going to be taken off the island because the Russians thought they were spies."

Erik just shook his head. "Spies. Since the war ended, these Russians have been looking for something to do. But this is ridiculous."

"What would you suggest we do?" asked Uncle Morten. "You know the island."

The teenager looked out a window at the pier. "That's why I

came, only I was going to take you to another place."

"Where?" asked Henrik.

Erik just kept shaking his head. "Doesn't matter now. Maybe this is better. Finish your breakfast, and then I'll take you to the Castle. We'll see if your Russian friend was right."

They hungrily finished their food, then cleaned up and packed their small bags once more. Henrik was the first to start up the stairs to the wheelhouse, but Erik grabbed his arm.

"Not so fast," he warned. "The guards are out there again. The Castle is just across town, but first we have to lose these two fellows."

"That means we'll separate," suggested Uncle Morten, and Erik nodded.

"The place we're going overlooks the harbor on the other side." Erik pointed toward the far end of the harbor. "But let's start out as if we're going back to the hotel, then separate and get back together."

The others nodded, and they started up the ladder.

"There they are," said Peter when he saw the soldiers standing in the shadows of the pier warehouse. An overhead streetlight in the distance managed to cast only a faint light on the two men. "Same place they were before."

"Don't point," warned Elise, buttoning up her coat as they stepped out into the cool morning air. It didn't seem as cold as before, but the two soldiers still kept their fur hats pressed down tightly on their heads.

Erik looked straight at the soldiers and smiled. "Good morning!" he called out.

One of the soldiers, the big gorilla who had met them when they first landed, smiled and nodded back. But the other guard scowled and poked his friend with his elbow while he whispered something to him.

"Watch," said Erik quietly. "They'll give us about twenty steps, and then they'll follow us."

Peter counted to twenty-five after they walked past the pair of guards, then looked back over his shoulder.

"You were right," said Peter. "Here they come."

"Act as if they're not there," Erik told them. "Then when we get up to this corner, I'll say good-bye, but you come with me, Mr. Andersen. You kids go the opposite direction, and if one of the guards follows you, lose him. We'll meet back at the Saint Nikolai Church. The big white one back there by the harbor. Got it?"

Henrik and the twins nodded.

"All right with you, Mr. Andersen?" asked the teenager. "It should be getting light in another half hour or so."

Uncle Morten ran his hand across his blond beard, thinking. "All right, but after this I'm going up to the hotel to speak with Captain Ivanov again."

"He's never going to tell you anything," insisted Erik. By that time, they had reached the corner, and he took Peter's hand to shake it.

"Nice to see you again," said Erik in a loud, slow voice. "Have a happy Christmas."

"Christmas?" Somehow Peter had forgotten about the holiday. He grinned and returned the greeting. "Oh, right. It's Christmas Day. Sure doesn't seem like it."

Erik smiled broadly and made a show of waving to Henrik and Elise while he whispered to them through his smile. "Remember the white church. Meet by the front door."

Peter, Elise, and Henrik waved once more and turned to the right while Uncle Morten and Erik turned the opposite direction, toward the hotel. Out of the corner of his eye, Peter saw the two soldiers hesitate in the dim light from a shop window. The smaller one set off after Uncle Morten and Erik, while the big guard stayed behind.

"Hey, wait a minute," said Peter. He turned and ran back along the pier while the guard backed up a couple of steps and watched him curiously. Peter hurried up to the little *Anna Marie* and swung on board.

"Have to check to see if Tiger showed up last night," he yelled back at the others. But it only took a moment to see that the meat scraps in the bowl were untouched. Peter stared at the food, frowned, and looked straight at the guard, who stood only a few feet away.

"Hey, mister," began Peter, taking a deep breath. "I lost my cat. Cat?"

Peter made an outline of two pointed ears on top of his head and then meowed. "Cat?"

"Ahh," said the big man, rocking back on his heels and smiling. He was obviously enjoying the performance. "*Koshka.*"

"Right," said Peter, nodding quickly. "Cat. Koshka." He pointed to himself. "My koshka. My cat." Then Peter pointed around the harbor area, pointed to himself again and began calling out, "Koshka! Koshka!"

"Da," said the friendly guard, looking around. "Koshka."

Peter nodded, while Henrik came closer and yelled at him from a distance.

"Peter, are you coming?" The Russian was still laughing and repeating Peter's imitation of a cat while Peter waved and followed Henrik back to where Elise was waiting.

"He was talking to the Russian," reported Henrik in a disgusted tone, hurrying down the street. "They were doing charades or something."

"Well, I thought maybe that big guy might . . ." Peter gave up trying to explain and just hurried after Henrik. The twins followed him up a street called Harbor Hill as fast as they could, past a row of bombed-out shops. In the morning darkness, they seemed to be the only ones awake.

"Don't look back," warned Henrik, "but your friend has decided to follow us."

They turned right around a corner, then Henrik scrambled over a pile of bricks into what had probably once been a store of some kind. The walls were still up, but the roof was gone and shelves were buried under piles of splintered boards.

"Watch out for the broken glass," whispered Elise, ducking down behind a window.

They stood still in the building, listening for the footsteps of the big guard as he ran to catch up. Henrik pointed as the Russian rounded the corner, then the footsteps stopped. Peter held his breath until they started again, heading away from them down the side street.

"That was too easy," said Peter, getting up from behind a ceiling beam that had fallen on the shop's floor. A streetlight cast crazy shadows in the ruined building where they stood.

"Maybe," agreed Henrik, "but let's get going back down the hill before he turns around."

Peter started for the entrance they had come through, only to see it blocked by a stern-looking man with wild hair and taped-together black glasses. He wore wooden clogs, wrinkled black pants, and a red-striped bathrobe over his white T-shirt. By the expression on the man's face, Peter thought he'd rather meet the Russian guard.

"I told you kids I'd call the police if I ever caught you playing in my store again," he spat out in his thick island accent. Peter strained to understand. "And now here on Christmas Day. Why aren't you at home where you belong?"

"Please, sir," began Elise. "We've never been here before. Maybe you think we're someone else. We're just visiting the island for Christmas."

Elise's speech obviously gave her away as an off-islander. The man unfolded his arms and put his hands on his hips instead.

"That's right," Henrik chimed in. "We are staying on Mr. Torp's boat down in the harbor."

Peter tried to look through a hole in the wall down the street in the direction the Russian guard had disappeared. The guard would have given up chasing them by that time and would probably turn around and walk back the way he had come.

"You're a friend of Uffe Torp?" asked the man, still not convinced. "Well, even if you are, you have no business playing in my store."

"We're awfully sorry, sir," offered Peter. "We didn't know we weren't supposed to. . . ."

"Well, I think you could have used your heads. This isn't a place for tourists, you know."

"No, sir," said Henrik. "We're sorry."

The angry shopkeeper reluctantly stepped aside to let the kids pass. "I won't call the police this time, but you kids stay out of bombed-out buildings from now on, you hear?"

"Yes, sir." Elise nodded.

Peter hurried past the man, stepping on Elise's heels. When they reached the sidewalk, they turned left while Peter glanced down the street to the right.

"It's the Russian!" he yelped, breaking into a run.

They streaked down Harbor Hill, passing a man out walking his cocker spaniel. Instantly the dog panicked and tugged on its leash to get out of the way. Henrik hurdled expertly over the little cream-colored dog.

"This way," he called to the twins, halfway down the hill. Peter looked over his shoulder; the soldier was still out of sight, or at least he couldn't see anyone in the little pools of light from streetlights.

"He's still way back there," observed Elise. But just to make sure they would lose him again, they followed Henrik through a zigzag pattern behind several destroyed shops, down another street, and around the block to where they could make out the green copper roof of what had to be the Saint Nikolai Church, the one Erik had told them about.

"Where are they?" asked Peter when they shuffled up to the church. "Erik said to meet by the front door, didn't he?"

"That's what I said," chimed in Erik, coming up behind them with Uncle Morten. "But we were beginning to wonder what happened to you kids."

"Did you have any troubles?" asked Uncle Morten.

Peter was still catching his breath from running. He looked around the open area in front of the church and pointed toward the place where Harbor Hill Street started—a stone's throw from where they stood. "Kind of, but not really. It's just that the guard who chased us is probably going to come running down the hill right about now."

Erik nodded and looked at Uncle Morten as someone from inside the church opened the big wooden double doors behind them. A young man with a flash of black hair and a pastor's white collar looked up in surprise when he saw them. "Oh! You're a little early for Christmas Day services, Erik. . . ."

Erik smiled and backed down the steps. "I'll be back later, Pastor Lassen."

The teenager didn't pause long enough to introduce them, but Erik waved as they hurried down the rest of the hill to follow the harbor road.

"Is that where you go to church, Erik?" asked Elise.

Erik nodded. "Pastor Lassen is terrific. Maybe you'll get a chance to meet him before you leave."

They hurried past the small boat harbor, where a mixed collection of workboats, fishing boats, and a couple of battered sailboats bobbed together behind a stone breakwater. On another day, Peter would have liked to stop and look, but they hurried on.

"The Castle is up here," said Erik, pointing around a bend in the road and to the left, up the hill again. Toward the crest of the wooded hill, Peter could make out the squat, powerful-looking tower. It wasn't particularly tall, maybe three or four stories from top to bottom, but it looked solid. A pinkish yellow glow from behind the tower told them that the sun was coming up.

"That's not a castle at all," said Henrik. "Looks more like a fort."

"That's just what they've always called it," replied Erik. "It's really old—from the sixteen hundreds. I think the old Bornholmers figured they could defend the whole island from up there. They could fire their cannon out that little row of windows on the top."

Peter looked up at the single row of windows along the top of the round tower, just under a cone-shaped peak.

"Did it work?" he asked.

"See for yourself." Erik waved his hand toward the Castle. "First the Germans took the place, and now the Russians."

Even from a distance, Peter could make out the deep red Soviet flag waving from a white flagpole in front of a small building next to the Castle. Several cars were parked in front, but no one was in sight. As they watched, the sun peeked out from behind the tower.

"Looks like a picture postcard," said Elise.

"What's the building?" asked Uncle Morten.

"Just a temporary headquarters the Russians put up," replied Erik. "They have camps for most of their men in the middle of the island, but I think the military leaders wanted their own place closer to the harbor. If your Russian friend was right, this is where your people are."

Henrik looked anxiously at Uncle Morten, as if waiting for a command to attack.

"That's where my mother is?" he whispered.

Uncle Morten hesitated in the middle of the quiet road, then pulled them off to the side. "We're not just going to go charging in there. Let's watch for a while."

Henrik sighed but stood still in the middle of the road. Somewhere behind them, Peter heard a car approaching.

"Come on, Henrik," he told his friend, grabbing his arm. "Car coming!"

The five of them hurried for the bushes at the side of the road and managed to duck under cover just before an old gray car rounded the corner and wheezed up the slope. Peter wondered if the people inside would have to jump out and help push the car up the hill, but then the driver shifted gears and the car jerked slowly up to the building.

"That's Ivanov's car," whispered Erik, but they couldn't make out who was inside.

Henrik and the twins watched the car carefully as it parked in front of the Russian headquarters. With the morning sun now squarely in his face, Peter squinted and cupped his hands around his eyes like a pair of binoculars to try to see who was stepping out of the car. First the driver jumped out, then the familiar figure of the Russian captain got out of the passenger's side.

"Is that Ivanov?" asked Henrik.

Erik nodded.

"What are we going to do?" asked Henrik, pacing nervously behind a cluster of birch trees.

Uncle Morten crossed his arms while he looked up and down the street. "We wait until we see someone bring them in. That's what the man said, wasn't it? Maybe they're coming a little later."

Henrik looked at Peter and Elise, who both nodded.

"Sometime this morning," said Peter. "All he said was sometime this morning."

"Well, now I believe you," whispered Erik, pointing back at the building. "Looks like they're pulling a woman out of the backseat."

"Mother!" gasped Henrik, getting to his feet. Instantly Erik yanked Henrik back down.

"Let me go!" Henrik tried to push the older boy away, but Erik sat on Henrik and gripped his shoulders.

"Hush!" commanded Erik. "If you want to get your mother back, you can't go charging up to the Castle like that."

Uncle Morten kneeled by the two boys while Peter and Elise looked for something they could do. Erik was right, but Peter couldn't just stand by and do nothing. He looked quickly up at the building but saw only a soldier disappearing into the front door with someone who looked like Matthias.

"All right, Erik," said Uncle Morten. "It's okay. Henrik, you need to stay with us, all right?"

Henrik nodded, but Peter could see tears in his eyes. "But we're so close. We can't just let them take her into the building without saying anything."

Uncle Morten glanced back up the hill. "They just did. Now at least we have proof."

"Did she look hurt to you?" asked Elise. "Remember what the man said on the phone?"

Uncle Morten shook his head. "I couldn't tell."

As they stood wondering what to do, Captain Ivanov stepped out of the building and climbed back into the car. His driver followed, and a moment later, they were coasting down the hill. Peter and the others pulled back once more into the bushes.

"Now maybe we can go back to that Ivanov character and get the straight story," decided Uncle Morten.

"But why don't we just go up there?" insisted Henrik, pointing back at the Russian building.

Erik stood up and offered Henrik his hand. "That's the worst thing you could do, at least right now. I think we're going to need help."

"Help?" Uncle Morten gave him a puzzled look.

"Come on," said the teenager. "I'll tell you while we're walking back to the hotel."

DANGEROUS VOYAGE

By late morning, the Mission Hotel's little restaurant was much quieter than the night before, with most of the tables empty. When they walked in, Evy came up to them with a smile.

"We're supposed to be closed today," she told them jokingly. "Actually we are, but our Russian friends don't seem to care." She glanced back at the far corner where Captain Ivanov sat at his usual table, sipping a cup of coffee and reading a Russian newspaper.

"He just got here ten minutes ago," she whispered. "Did you find out anything?"

Erik nodded seriously and disappeared into the kitchen with his cousin. Uncle Morten set his jaw and stepped through the restaurant to face the Russian captain, the twins and Henrik in tow.

"Captain Ivanov?" demanded Uncle Morten, drawing himself up next to the captain's table.

The Russian looked up casually and put down his cup of coffee.

"Ah, An-day-son," said the captain. He pointed at a chair next to him. "An-day-son kids. Sit?"

That was more Danish all at once than Peter had heard from the man before. Uncle Morten shook his head and kept his arms crossed, though, forcing Captain Ivanov to look up again. Peter held on to his uncle's belt.

"We believe we've seen Mrs. Melchior," announced Uncle Morten, clearing his throat. He pointed to his eyes and then in the direction of the Castle, trying to use sign language. "Mrs. Melchior."

The captain, smiling with his ever-so-crooked teeth, just shook his head. He took his spoon and tapped on a drinking glass, like a bell for a servant. "Sit, An-day-son. Sit."

Almost like a genie, Lieutenant Riznik appeared behind them. Another man in a wrinkled suit was with him.

"Comrade Riznik," said the captain, then he let loose with a torrent of Russian. The little translator slipped into his position next to the captain, nodding, while the captain gestured. For a second, Peter tried to imagine him as the mysterious man who had visited them on the boat to tell them about Henrik's mother. The man in the wrinkled suit, pink-faced and middle-aged, took a seat across from Captain Ivanov.

"Eh, the captain says that you should sit down and tell him what is on your mind," said Lieutenant Riznik, still standing. He seemed nervous and would not look directly at Uncle Morten or the rest of them. "And this is Sergeant Olsen from the island's police."

Uncle Morten took a step back. "I'm glad you're here, Sergeant. We're here to ask the Russians if they have any news about Mrs. Melchior, the boy's mother. She was—"

"Yes, I'm afraid I've heard the story," the Danish man interrupted, sounding apologetic. "We have no reports of anyone landing a plane on the island, and the Russians say they know of nothing."

"Well . . . yes," Uncle Morten stammered. "That's what the Russians say, but can't you check into it?"

"I'm afraid there's really nothing I can do, unless you want to come into my office the day after tomorrow and file a complaint. I'm really not on duty right now, and, besides, it appears to be a military matter."

Captain Ivanov seemed amused as he sipped his coffee and

listened to the translation. Then he pointed at his cup and raised his eyebrows.

"*Cofeeyeh?*" he asked, using a word that sounded to Peter as if he were clearing his throat.

Uncle Morten shook his head while the Russian captain whispered to his lieutenant.

"Captain Ivanov says that, unfortunately, he still has no news about the woman or her friend, except to tell you again that they are not on the island."

"He's lying," hissed Henrik, stepping out from behind Uncle Morten. "Tell him that we saw him with her, and that we know where she is!"

"Henrik," scolded Uncle Morten. "Let me do the talking, please." He turned back to Captain Ivanov and the other men. "What the boy meant was that—"

But Captain Ivanov raised his hand, cutting him off. He looked curiously at his translator as Lieutenant Riznik told him what Henrik had said. Peter put a hand on his friend's shoulder while Captain Ivanov returned a stormy reply, his eyes suddenly blazing.

"Captain Ivanov says, eh . . ." The translator gulped while his captain made a stirring motion with his hand for him to continue. "He says he has never met this woman you are looking for and that you did not see any Mrs. Melchior because there is no Mrs. Melchior on the island. And if you did think you saw her, the captain wants to know where that would be?"

Uncle Morten hesitated, and Peter looked down to see Henrik clenching his fist.

"Perhaps it was nothing," replied Uncle Morten, suddenly sounding apologetic himself.

"What?" gasped Henrik.

Peter couldn't understand why his uncle was saying this, but he kept quiet.

Captain Ivanov seemed to relax at the answer, flashing his crooked smile once more and saying something to the translator.

"The captain says he is glad," continued Riznik, "or rather, that it is unfortunate you have not found her here. Then he says that you will be leaving right away on your boat, and that as a Christmas gift the Russian army will fill up your tanks with fuel so you can leave immediately. He insists."

"Tell the captain he is very generous," said Uncle Morten. "We'll leave as soon as the tanks are full. Good-bye, gentlemen."

Uncle Morten turned to go, trying to corral the twins and Henrik with his arms. But Peter stood frozen in place, shocked at what his uncle was saying. Henrik's face turned red.

How can Uncle Morten do this? Peter wanted to know. *Why is he giving up so easily?*

He looked up at his uncle's face and saw a hint of a wink. "Trust me," whispered Uncle Morten, barely moving his lips. Peter made sure that Elise had heard as they all shuffled through the restaurant to the kitchen door.

"See you at the prayer meeting tonight," whispered Erik from behind the swinging door. Peter waved but didn't dare look back into the restaurant, where he heard Captain Ivanov laughing.

Elise whispered into her brother's ear as they left the building. "Did he say prayer meeting? What prayer meeting?"

"I know you're wondering what's going on," Uncle Morten told them as they walked back to the boat. They hurried to keep up with his pace through the quiet streets. "Especially you, Henrik."

Henrik kicked at a rock in the street. "Am I the only one who's confused?"

"I wanted to see if he would tell us the truth," continued Uncle Morten. "But Erik was right. They're not going to tell us anything, and it wouldn't have done any good to make a scene there in front of the police. So our plan is to leave the island, just like the Russians want us to."

"Leave?" asked Henrik. "But what about that guy on the boat this morning? He said they're going to take Mother away tomorrow."

"Don't worry, Henrik. We'll be right back. You didn't hear everything that Erik and I worked out. I've already arranged with

Erik to meet us on the other side of the island after dark."

"That won't be long," said Peter. "It's been getting dark at three-thirty."

"And what was all that about a prayer meeting?" Elise wanted to know.

Uncle Morten gave them a smile as they neared the fishing boat where they had slept the night before. "Hope you don't mind. I told Erik we'd come. He and Evy have some friends who can help. . . ."

He stopped explaining when he saw the two guards back at their places by the warehouse. Henrik groaned.

"It's our two friends again," said Peter.

"Okay, don't worry about a thing," Uncle Morten told them. "One thing I hadn't planned on was that we would get a free tank of gas out of the deal. Now we just need to get our stuff back to the *Anna Marie* and make sure it gets fueled up so we can leave."

Captain Ivanov wasted no time with the fuel. Almost before they had walked back to their little boat with their bags, they saw a horse-drawn wagon with three Russian soldiers. All three were no more than teenagers, and they laughed and chatted as they pulled up next to the *Anna Marie*.

"Benzín?" asked the teen holding the reins. Finally, here was one of the few words that was the same in both Russian and Danish.

"Gasoline?" repeated Uncle Morten. "Right here." He pointed to the top of the fuel-filler pipe on the deck next to the wheelhouse. Then he showed them how to unscrew the top with a wrench and watched as the three Russians took turns carrying large metal cans full of gas to the boat.

"Make sure they don't spill those heavy cans," Uncle Morten told Peter and Henrik. "They need to use the funnel. Elise, why don't you come with me to get the rest of our stuff from the *Cecilie*."

"Elise," added Peter. "Can you be sure to bring my Bible back, too? I think it's . . ." He paused, trying to think of a way to say it without embarrassing Henrik. "It's probably on the floor somewhere, maybe in one of our rooms."

"Sure," replied his sister. "I'll find it."

While Elise and Uncle Morten were gone, Peter and Henrik took turns holding the funnel as the teens slowly poured fuel into their tank. Every once in a while, the Russians would try to say something to them, loudly and slowly, as if that would make a difference.

"Sorry," Peter tried to tell one of them, a taller boy who seemed to be the leader of the three. "The only Russian words I know are *da, nyet,* and *koshka.*"

"Koshka?" asked the Russian with a toothy smile.

Peter just shook his head and smiled. "I'm not going to act it out for you like I did with the big guy. But if you see Tiger, I wish you'd tell me."

"These guys don't understand a word you're saying, Peter," said Henrik, balancing his side of the funnel.

"Yeah, I know. But they don't seem so bad. I'll bet they don't have any idea what's going on with your mom."

"Maybe not," answered Henrik, concentrating on holding the funnel.

"Hey, slow down," Henrik warned a couple of minutes later as the gas slipped over the edge of the funnel and sloshed onto the deck. "Peter, go grab a rag."

"Right." Peter jumped to his feet just as he heard a splash in the water from the other side of the boat. He looked over to see one of the older Russian guards slipping out of the other side of the wheelhouse.

"Hey," yelled Peter. "What were you doing in there?"

At first the guard tried to ignore the question. He wasn't holding anything, and Peter couldn't see anything down in the water either.

"Did you drop something?" asked Peter, not expecting an answer. "There's nothing in there to steal, if that's what you're looking for."

"Cigarette?" asked the soldier, making a smoking motion with his hand.

Peter shook his head, plugged his nose, and made a face. "We don't have any cigarettes. *Nyet* cigarette."

The guard shrugged and jumped off the boat onto the pier, but still Peter felt uneasy. What had the man dropped into the water?

After he found a rag for Henrik, he went back inside, looking for anything that was missing. The floorboards to the engine room were out of place, but they could already have been that way. Other than that, he could find nothing wrong.

"Almost done, boys?" asked Uncle Morten, stepping back on the boat.

"Five more of those big gas cans to pour in," reported Henrik. "I think there were ten."

"Good," nodded Uncle Morten. He stepped into the wheel-house and pulled out a chart from a shelf on the wall next to the big wooden steering wheel. "We'll get under way by one, then."

"Can you show us where we're going?" asked Elise.

Uncle Morten looked around carefully. The three teenagers were still pouring gas with Henrik, but the two guards had disappeared. Peter helped his uncle unroll the chart and lay it flat against the small counter by the front window.

"Here's where we are." Uncle Morten pointed with a pencil at Ronne Harbor, which was at the lower left corner of the roughly square island. "We're starting out here in Ronne, and we're going to head north this way, the same way we would go if we were going home. But in a couple of hours, it will be dark, so we can turn right around, go back the way we came, and this time sail right past Ronne to the next harbor."

"Arnager?" asked Elise, reading the name of the little town on the map. It was just a few miles past the airport, on the same road they had traveled with Erik and Evy that first night. The south side of the island.

Uncle Morten thumped the map with his finger at the little harbor town. "Arnager. I've arranged for Erik and Evy to meet us there."

Peter put his nose to the map, trying to read the numbers that showed how deep the water was.

"Doesn't look like much of a harbor," he said.

"Erik says it's full of rocks," answered Uncle Morten. "Only the locals know how to get through the shallow water, so Erik is going to meet us at the mouth of the channel in a rowboat at five-thirty tonight and lead us in."

"And then what?" wondered Elise.

"That's the part we're not quite sure about. But we're working on it."

Elise looked out at Henrik, who was still holding the funnel for the Russian teenagers pouring gas. "Do you know what Erik meant about having a prayer meeting?"

"A prayer meeting," said Uncle Morten, patting her on the back and rolling up the map. "That's the best idea I've heard yet. Are you kids ready to go?"

"As soon as we find something to eat," answered Peter, thinking back to the light breakfast of bread and cheese they had on Uffe Torp's big fishing boat.

"Hey, are you guys talking about having something to eat?" yelled Henrik, still holding the funnel. "I'm starving."

Elise wrinkled her nose as they walked by him. "Ooh," she teased. "You smell like you're ready to go to the best restaurant in town, with that gasoline cologne."

In the distance, toward the town, Peter thought he saw the familiar, stooped outline of their Christmasman, Uffe Torp. He was shuffling toward his boat with a large box in his arms.

"Look who's coming," announced Elise.

Mr. Torp must have spotted them at the same time because he waved at them to join him and nearly dropped his load. By the time they were back on Uffe's big boat, Henrik had joined them, too.

"I smell it," he said. "Do you?"

Peter couldn't smell a thing, but they followed Uncle Morten aboard.

"Come on down!" boomed their host.

When they climbed down the ladder, Uffe Torp was pulling out plates and cups and arranging them around the wooden fold-up table in the center of the main room.

"I thought you might like a bite to eat before you, ah, leave."

The little man looked up at them and winked. "Wouldn't want you to be hungry for your long trip."

"Wow," said Henrik as he looked at the food being set out. "I don't think we will be. Roast goose!"

"Just a few leftovers from Christmas dinner at the hotel," said the old man, grinning. "There's a little bit of roast goose, some potatoes, red cabbage, gravy, even a few rolls."

"This is too much, Mr. Torp," protested Uncle Morten.

"Oh, is it?" asked the old man. He picked up the bowl of red cabbage. "That's fine. I'll just take it back."

"But then again . . ." Uncle Morten smiled at the way Uffe Torp teased them as he sat down. "You'll make it seem like Christmas after all, the way you're treating us."

Peter looked over at his uncle, expecting him to pray for the meal, but Mr. Torp beat them to it.

"Father in heaven," he began, as if he was talking to someone right there at the table. Everyone bowed their heads, even Henrik. "We thank you for this special food you have given us, and we thank you for the way you always answer prayer. We pray that you will be with the Andersens and Henrik, bringing them back safely, and that you will work tonight in a mighty way. In Jesus' name. Amen."

Peter looked up from praying, waiting for someone to explain what was going on that night, but old Mr. Torp and Uncle Morten just started to pass around the bowls of food. Henrik rolled the drumstick onto his plate before Peter could reach it, then cleared his throat.

"Um, does this mean that we're coming back?" asked Henrik. Peter almost forgot that Henrik hadn't already heard Uncle Morten explain what they were doing.

Mr. Torp looked at Uncle Morten. "So you haven't told them?"

Uncle Morten finished chewing a mouthful of red cabbage, then lowered his voice. "I mentioned it to the twins, but Henrik hasn't heard."

"Well then, let me tell you the whole story," replied Mr. Torp. "We've asked around the church, and we thought that tonight might be the perfect time for an old-fashioned Christmas sing-along. A few people from our prayer group . . ."

Peter's mind wandered to Tiger, still lost somewhere in the strange city. Why hadn't he come back? Old Mr. Torp continued talking, then stopped.

"I said, more goose, Peter?" Mr. Torp waved his hand in front of Peter's face. Peter sat up straight and tried to smile.

"Oh, I'm sorry. I must have drifted off for a second."

"He's worried about his cat," said Elise.

"Cat?" asked the old man. "Back home?"

"No " answered Peter. He explained how Tiger had come along and then disappeared on the island. Mr. Torp nodded his head in understanding.

"We'll keep an eye out for your Tiger," he said. "But if he hasn't come back by now, I'm afraid it doesn't sound good."

Mr. Torp was interrupted by the rocking of his boat, a sure sign that someone had just stepped aboard. "Is someone here?" he asked, wiping his mouth with a napkin.

Peter heard heavy steps above his head.

"Hallo, An-day-son?" came a voice from up in the wheelhouse.

Uncle Morten closed his eyes. "Sounds like our Russian friends again."

Not waiting for an invitation, Captain Ivanov and his translator came clattering down the steps as Uncle Morten and Mr. Torp got to their feet.

"Oh, sorry to interrupt your meal," said Lieutenant Riznik as he helped Captain Ivanov down the last step. "But the captain was anxious to find you."

Uncle Morten nodded while Captain Ivanov talked at them in Russian. He never stopped staring at Uncle Morten, as if the Danish man could understand what he was saying.

"Captain Ivanov says to tell you," translated Lieutenant Riznik, "that he just wanted to make sure you received your fuel and that everything would be prepared for you to leave."

"Tell your captain that we are grateful for your help and that we will be ready to leave as soon as I finish my goose."

The captain listened for a minute, nodded, and then smiled while Uncle Morten found a scrap of paper and a pencil in a small rack behind the table.

"And please tell the captain," continued Uncle Morten, scribbling something on the paper, "that if he finds out anything about our missing friends to please have you call us at this number in Helsingor."

"Of course," said the lieutenant, taking the paper and bowing slightly before they turned and headed back up the ladder.

Peter watched the two Russian officers through a porthole as they stepped off the fishing boat. Lieutenant Riznik handed Uncle Morten's paper to the captain. As they walked down the pier together, the captain laughed, wadded up the paper, and tossed it into the harbor.

Less than an hour later, Uncle Morten was piloting them carefully out of Ronne Harbor, the pale yellow winter sun low in the sky ahead of them over the ocean.

"Are they watching us?" asked Henrik. Peter had the binoculars and was studying the shore behind them.

"Captain Ivanov just showed up again and he's talking to the two guards," replied Peter. He put down the binoculars and gave his sister a worried look. "I don't like it."

Elise crossed her arms as the boat began to rock up and down in the ocean swells. "They don't know what we're doing, and we don't know what they're doing. I wonder if that makes us even?"

"We'll be even when I get my mother back," said Henrik, looking ahead into the silvery gray ocean.

"And my cat," finished Peter. But as they slowly pulled away from the island, he tried to get used to the idea that Tiger was really gone.

Why didn't you come back, boy? We looked for you as much as we could before we had to leave, but you never came. What happened to you?

Peter pressed the binoculars to his eyes until they hurt, trying to catch one last glimpse of the harbor. But it was getting harder and harder to see in the fading light, and the binocular eyepiece had fogged up, anyway.

"If I saw Tiger now, could we turn around to get him, Uncle Morten?" Peter tried one more time.

Uncle Morten sighed but didn't answer, and kept them pointed toward the Danish mainland at an unusually slow, steady pace. A couple of seagulls followed them for a ways, then gave up when they decided there would be no food for them from the little fishing boat. Peter closed his stinging eyes but kept the binoculars to his face so Elise wouldn't see his tears.

Good-bye, Tiger. Take care of yourself, wherever you are.

After Peter slowly put the binoculars away, he and Elise stationed themselves on either side of the steering wheel while Uncle Morten studied his map.

"I tell you what, kids," he finally announced. "We're going to just keep on this course, northwest, at this slow speed, until dark." He glanced at his watch. "That's only a couple more hours. We don't want to get too far out before we turn around and head for Arnager Harbor."

Henrik looked around. Behind them, Bornholm Island was a large hump in the distance. From somewhere over the island, something that looked like another seagull seemed to lift from the middle of the land and come their way. Henrik pointed.

"I think it's a plane," he said excitedly.

They all watched as the speck grew larger.

"I think you're right," agreed Peter. "But it's moving awfully fast."

As they watched, the plane streaked in their direction, coming low over the water.

"Russian?" wondered Peter.

Henrik nodded.

"Looks like they're coming to check up on us," reported Uncle Morten as the silver-gray military fighter plane roared almost overhead to the right. As it passed by, the pilot banked to the left, showing a single red star on the side of the plane. Peter could see someone inside, but the pilot didn't wave or even look to the side.

"It's Russian," agreed Peter. Elise held her hands to her ears while the plane turned in front of them and returned to the island.

"Yeah," said Henrik. "You can tell because he's so friendly."

Uncle Morten frowned and watched the plane as it returned to the island. "They're making sure that we're really going home, aren't they?"

"Looks that way," said Elise.

"Okay, Peter," said Uncle Morten, handing over the wheel to him. "It looks like the excitement is over. If there's anything else, you can wake me. I'm going to try to get a little nap before we turn back."

Peter looked at the compass. "Same course?"

"Same course until it's dark, but no later. Then wake me up if I'm still asleep."

Peter nodded and looked at his sister and Henrik. "We can take turns steering."

Uncle Morten nodded and slipped back to the little bunk in the back of the wheelhouse. Peter wondered how his uncle would be able to take a nap with the noise from the engine. But after a few minutes, the rocking of the ocean waves made his own eyelids flutter, too.

"Think the Russians are going to come back?" wondered Henrik, looking back at the island.

Henrik's question was answered a half hour later when the Russian plane repeated its loop around the little fishing boat.

"They're sure keeping an eye on us," said Elise. She was trying to draw some pictures on her sketch pad, but the light was low, and the rocking from the boat made Peter's stomach feel funny at the thought.

"I don't know how you can draw while we're moving like this," he told her as the little *Anna Marie* pushed through the waves. Elise just smiled and held up a drawing of a Christmas tree. Above the tree was a bright star, its rays shining. Peter gave her a thumbs-up sign.

The seas were just the way Peter liked them: mostly calm, but with a little chop to make it interesting. Once in a while, the boat would rise up on a couple of waves and throw a little spray, and Peter would have to wrestle the big steering wheel around to get the boat back on course. He looked down at the *Anna Marie*'s compass and steered around to keep them on a course of three hundred twenty degrees. Northwest, in the direction of home.

While Elise continued drawing, Henrik stared out the back window in the direction of the island, thinking his own thoughts. Uncle Morten napped for another hour, the sky darkened to a deep reddish purple, and the Russian plane buzzed overhead again, as if to remind them to keep going home.

"So do we really know what's going on tonight?" Elise broke away from her drawing to watch the plane circle overhead before it returned once more in the direction of the island.

"I wish I knew," answered Peter. "Erik is going to meet us at Arnager Harbor, and then there's some kind of Christmas sing-along."

Henrik shook his head and started counting on his fingers. "What is it about these people? First they help us find the plane. Then they give us a place to stay and help us find Mother. Now they're going to help us get her back? They don't even know us!"

"Hmm," said Peter, steering a little to the right to slide down a wave. He tried to think how he could answer his friend without sounding like a preacher.

"And another thing, Peter," continued Henrik before Peter could think of what to say.

"Yeah?" squeaked Peter.

"I was reading your Bible last night after everyone was asleep."

Peter caught his breath. "I know."

"You know?" Henrik sputtered.

"Well, I couldn't sleep. I don't know what time it was, but I saw you reading."

It was quiet for a few minutes . . . only the sound of the engine and the waves. Elise was leaning against the window on the other side of the wheelhouse.

"What did you read?" Peter finally asked.

"The rest of that Hebrews letter Mr. Torp had made me read aloud. Took me a while to get through it."

"What'd you think?"

"I liked it, I think. A lot of it didn't make sense. Some of it did. And some parts kind of reminded me of my dad's letter, I guess."

Peter didn't know what else to ask, so he kept steering their course.

"The part in there about the prisoners was pretty good," Henrik continued, his voice barely loud enough to hear above the engine. " 'Remember those in prison as if you were their fellow prisoners.' Just like Mother."

"What about Matthias?" asked Peter, and he instantly regretted mentioning the man's name. No telling how Henrik would react.

"Yeah, I guess it reminds me of Matthias, too," said Henrik after a few seconds. "Maybe . . ."

Peter was afraid to ask anything more. But for the first time, Henrik hadn't said the man's name as if it were a curse. Something had begun to melt. Peter wondered if Elise had heard anything they had been saying.

"Peter . . ." Elise interrupted the silence. "Is it getting rougher out there?"

By that time, the sea around them had turned an inky black to match the sky. It didn't seem to Peter that the waves were any bigger, but something seemed different about the way the *Anna Marie* was behaving.

"I'm not sure," Peter finally answered. "Maybe we're kind of sloshing around more."

Elise stared out at the water a minute, then shook her head. "It still looks pretty calm to me. Doesn't it to you, Henrik?"

Henrik nodded. "Not bad. But I think it's time to turn around."

Uncle Morten snorted, slipped out of his bunk, and looked around. "You kids were supposed to wake me up when it got dark. Let's reverse course. Head back for the island and increase speed."

"Aye-aye," replied Peter, pushing up the throttle handle and spinning the wheel. But instead of turning sharply, as the *Anna Marie* usually did, the boat swayed wildly and quivered like a bowl of stiff pudding. Elise lost her balance and grabbed for the wall.

"Whoa!" said Uncle Morten. "What's going on out there? Feels like we have too many fish in the hold."

"Fish?" wondered Peter. He turned the handle of the throttle to go faster, but the boat only seemed to slouch down lower behind each little wave. Elise dropped to her knees and put her ear to the floorboards.

"There's water down there!" she cried. "It sounds like it's pouring in!"

Uncle Morten and Henrik jumped to help her, and together they pulled up one of the big floorboards, throwing it to the side. In the dim twilight, Peter stared down in horror at the ocean inside their little boat, black water filling the engine compartment almost a foot deep. Next to the engine, water was pouring in from some kind of hose, spraying like a city water fountain.

"Cut the engine!" shouted Uncle Morten as he jumped down next to the waterfall below. "Henrik, get me the flashlight. I can't see what's going on here."

Peter did as he was commanded, pressing against the side window as Henrik pushed past to get the flashlight in the emergency box bolted to the side wall.

"What is it?" he called down. "What happened?"

Uncle Morten fumbled around under the boat. "It's coming in somewhere, but I can't reach it! Henrik, where's that light?"

Henrik pounded on the flashlight with the palm of his hand and tried to switch it on and off, but nothing happened. "It's not working!" he told them, panic edging his voice. "Feels like the batteries are missing."

"I just put new ones in before we left," replied Uncle Morten. "Let's see it here."

Henrik obeyed, passing the useless light to Uncle Morten in the darkness. As the boat settled lower and lower into the waves, water washed over the front deck. The *Anna Marie* seemed to struggle back up for air only with a great effort.

One more wave like that, thought Peter, *and we're not going to make it*.

Without being told, Henrik and Elise pulled up another floorboard and threw it back onto the bunk. Henrik grabbed the handle of a pump and started pulling wildly.

"You're right about the batteries," said Uncle Morten, tossing the flashlight away in disgust. Henrik grunted as he pushed and pulled at the bilge pump, pumping water over the side with each grunt. It didn't seem to keep up with the water still coming in from below, but at least it was something.

"Okay, there are only two places this water could be coming from, Peter," said Uncle Morten. "The water comes in through the hull to cool the engine, then it goes back out. Do you know where those two places are? I can't reach the one that's on the other side, but I'll get the one that's down below."

Peter knew what his uncle was talking about, but in his panic, he couldn't think. The boat was sinking. Still, he slipped down beside his uncle, ready to help. The water was curiously warm, and almost up to his knees.

Peter tried to remember what the engine had looked like in the light. He had never paid much attention to it before, but he did remember how the hose for cooling water let ocean water in and pumped warm water out. Then he understood.

"It's got to be this hose over here," he told his uncle, wedging himself in next to the engine. "That's why the water is warm."

His uncle grunted from the other side of the engine. Peter reached down as far as he could, searching the side of the grimy engine.

"Can you reach it?" asked Uncle Morten, his voice cracking.

"Not yet." Peter knew he had to find where the water was coming in, and fast, or they might find themselves swimming in the dark. *Where is that hose?* He bit his lip.

"Peter!" said his sister.

"I know, I know," he replied. "I just can't . . ."

The water seemed even deeper than when he had first climbed down beside the engine. Then his hand closed around the hose.

"I found it!" he cried, following the hose from the engine. He could feel warm water rushing through the hose, and it wasn't hard to follow it to the end, where it was gushing out into the bottom of the boat. While Henrik kept up his pumping, Elise pulled away more floorboards so Uncle Morten could reach where Peter was struggling with the loose hose. Their uncle, dripping wet, reached across to help.

"It wasn't the other hose," he told Peter.

"Here's the one we're looking for," replied Peter. "Water's still pouring out of it."

"Good. Now let's find where it goes. Henrik, can you pump faster?"

By that time, Elise had joined Henrik at the pump, and together they pulled at the handle faster and faster and faster. Another wave knocked them from the side, and the little fishing boat seemed to turn in circles.

"Listen, I think I've got it," said Uncle Morten, pushing the hose back into place. Water sprayed all around them, soaking Henrik and Elise, as well. "I hope the engine will start up again, but it's so wet. Peter, get me a screwdriver, and then get ready to head us back into the waves."

Peter tried to climb back up, but another wave knocked them sideways. The water all shifted to the side, and the boat felt as if it would roll over.

"Quick, over to the high side!" yelled Uncle Morten. The floor had turned into a wall, and Peter, Elise, and Henrik all climbed up as high as they could. Peter buried his face in the floorboard, dug his fingernails into the painted wood, and closed his eyes, praying.

"Lord!" was all he had time to say while the boat teetered on its side. Time seemed to stand still as the water in the bottom of the boat poured out around their feet. Outside, another small wave smacked the side of the boat from behind them, nudging them back from the edge slowly, slowly. The wooden hull creaked and groaned.

"Come on," Henrik urged the boat. "You can do it."

Peter couldn't see his uncle down next to the engine, but he knew he had to be holding his breath under the wave of water. And still they hung there, suspended sideways.

"Uncle Morten?" whispered Elise.

There was no answer, until something finally seemed to pull the boat back from the edge. The little tidal wave that covered Uncle Morten began to slosh back in their direction, and a few seconds later, they were bobbing right side up once more.

"Screwdriver?" called Uncle Morten, breathing hard.

"Right," replied Peter, taking a deep breath and pulling himself off the floor. He found the tool in their emergency box and returned to his post by the steering wheel, while Henrik and Elise took up their pumping again. A minute later, Uncle Morten pulled himself out of the engine compartment, slammed down a floorboard, and clapped his hands together.

"Pray that it starts now," he told them, pulling himself up with a hand on Peter's shoulder. "Before another wave turns us over for good."

Peter felt for the starting button, took a deep breath, and pushed down hard with his palm.

RACE TO DANGER

For a moment, nothing happened, and Peter squeezed his eyes shut to keep from panicking.

"I was afraid of that," whispered their uncle. "The starter's probably flooded out. In fact, the whole engine may be flooded out. Under water. Elise, grab me the emergency flare out of the kit. Peter, you get the life jackets, and put one on yourself."

Peter reached under the bunk for the big cork life jackets stored there. But he knew that if they had to jump into the water, they wouldn't last long. This was December, after all, and they were in the middle of the icy Baltic.

"What's this?" he asked, pulling out a shredded piece of foam and a loose piece of cork. "The life jackets are all chopped up!"

From the other side of the wheelhouse, Elise had her own problem. "Uncle Morten," she announced, "I don't think there are any flares in here."

Peter remembered the splashes after the strange Russian soldier had come out of the boat, and it all fell into place. "I think I know what happened," he told them. "I saw one of those Russian guards coming out of the boat when we were filling up with gas.

I didn't know what he was doing, but I remember there was a splash, like he was throwing something off the boat."

"That figures." Uncle Morten kept pushing the starter, but still nothing happened. "The hose, the life jackets, the flares. Someone wanted us to get out here and not come back. But don't worry about that now. Peter, give Henrik a rest on that pump."

Peter took the pump handle, trying to keep the motion of the pump going. It was harder than he thought—up and down, pulling out just a little water, while the *Anna Marie* rolled dangerously.

"I'm going to see if we can throw out a sea anchor," said Uncle Morten, moving for the door. "Elise, why don't you try that starter a few more times?"

"Okay," replied Elise, her voice trembling. She took the wheel.

Pump faster! Peter commanded his arms, and he pumped until he thought his heart would burst.

"Maybe we can push start," said Henrik, "like we did that old taxi."

Peter had to smile. If Henrik was still making jokes, they still had a chance.

Out on the deck in the dark somewhere, they could hear Uncle Morten putting out his rope. A sea anchor dragging behind them would help them face into the waves. But before it had a chance to work, another set of larger waves hit from the side, and once more Peter felt the boat rolling dangerously.

"Not again!" cried Peter, gripping the handle tightly for balance. He heard his sister slap at the starter once more, then a whirring, grinding noise broke loose from somewhere below.

"There it is," announced Elise between clenched teeth. Peter held his breath and held on.

Suddenly the engine roared to life, but the *Anna Marie* was still rolling beneath the latest wave attack.

"Steer into the waves!" Peter shouted to his sister.

"To the right!" added Henrik.

Elise pulled hard to the right, and the boat swung slowly around to meet the waves, then began plowing straight ahead.

The waves washed over the low front deck, but at least the boat wasn't rolling.

"Does anyone see Uncle Morten?" asked Elise, staring out at the dark forward deck.

What if he fell overboard? worried Peter. He pressed his nose to the rear window and pounded on the glass, but nothing moved.

"He's not out there!" Peter shouted over the noise of the engine. "We've got to go back!"

Suddenly the door slammed, and Uncle Morten stumbled into the wheelhouse.

"I'm here, kids," he told them. "I guess the engine just needed a lady's touch."

"Uncle Morten!" gasped Peter. "What happened?"

"It was a bit of a wild ride," he answered. "Now let's get this little boat pumped out and hurry back to the island."

Henrik and Peter took turns on the pump while Elise steered and Uncle Morten scooped out as much water as he could with a bucket. Slowly the *Anna Marie* floated higher and higher, and Elise increased their speed as they neared the island until it seemed as if they were flying through the water. Uncle Morten spread his map out next to the compass and tried to track their position by the tiny red light that escaped from the glass case.

"So how did they sabotage the boat?" asked Henrik as he turned the pump handle over to Peter. He climbed into the bunk behind them; it was his turn to change into dry clothes.

"He probably loosened up the hose so the end was just barely hanging on," replied Peter. "When it finally shook loose, we started pumping water right into the boat."

"Maybe so," replied Uncle Morten. "We don't have any proof. Elise, keep steering southeast. One hundred thirty-five degrees on the compass."

Peter stopped pumping for a moment to catch his breath. "But didn't you say the hose was fine before, Uncle Morten?"

"I put it on myself," their uncle sighed. "I know it was safe."

Elise leaned forward in the darkness over the steering wheel. "I think I see lights up ahead."

"Good steering," replied Uncle Morten. "Let's see where we are."

"Flashing light there," Henrik called out as he buttoned up a wrinkled but dry shirt. "Every five seconds."

Peter couldn't see out from where he was still pumping the water.

"Green light over there," echoed Elise.

"Good." Uncle Morten rustled his map. "That's Ronne, where we came from. Just five more miles down the coast, and we'll hit Arnager Harbor. Let's hope the *Anna Marie* moved quickly enough to make up for lost time."

When it was Henrik's turn to pump once more, Peter studied the lights with his sister and Uncle Morten. Once in a while, they could make out the light from a house on the shore, but mostly the island was a dark shadow.

"Let's stay clear," said Uncle Morten. "Here, I'd better take the wheel now. Thanks, Elise."

Elise slumped back to the bunk behind them without a word.

"Are you okay, sis?" asked Peter, keeping his eyes on the lights from a farmhouse on a rise above the island's coast.

"Sure," she shot back, but the quiver in her voice gave her away.

She's just tired, Peter told himself, watching the cluster of lights up ahead grow closer. Arnager Harbor.

"Okay, now watch for something that looks like a flashlight," said Uncle Morten. "Erik said he would be waiting to guide us in past the rocks, only he was expecting us by five-thirty."

"Does someone see Erik?" asked Elise, jumping up from her bunk. "What time is it?"

Uncle Morten laughed. "I guess I mentioned the right name. It's nearly six, and no, we haven't seen Erik. But keep a lookout. Maybe he hasn't given up on us yet."

"I'm sure he hasn't," said Elise, staring out into the darkness with the rest of them.

"Is that it?" Peter finally asked, pointing to a small cluster of lights in the distance. Everyone else looked to see.

"I think so," Uncle Morten finally answered, double-checking his chart. "When we get a little closer, I'll blink our outside lights and see if Erik really did wait for us."

Uncle Morten cut their speed as they approached the lights, while Peter and Elise slipped out on deck to get a closer look. With the wind now behind them, from the south, somehow it wasn't as cold as Peter remembered. Still, they could see the white foam from waves crashing against rocks just ahead of them.

"I sure hope Erik is still here," muttered Peter, straining his eyes to make out the lights. "There's no way we're going to get into this little harbor without him."

"He'll be here," answered Elise. Peter didn't know how she could be so sure. But then Uncle Morten blinked their red and green lights, the ones mounted on the side of the cabin for night-time.

Elise looked back at the lights, then into the darkness ahead. "Now look for Erik's flashlight."

Peter's eyes started to ache from staring so hard, but still they saw nothing except the distant lights of the village. Then a dark shape—a rock, maybe—seemed to rise out of the black water ahead of them.

"Uncle Morten!" Peter shouted. "We're going to crash into a rock!"

CAROLING PARTY

Peter and Elise caught their balance on the railing of the boat as it jerked to a stop in a swirl of foam. Just ahead, Peter could see the white top of a wave washing over the rock they had almost met head on.

"Blink the lights again, Uncle Morten," called Elise.

This time Uncle Morten added a blast of his little horn for good measure, and they waited once again for an answering blink.

"There it is!" cried Elise, skipping back to the wheelhouse. "Straight ahead."

Peter stayed out on deck to follow the weak light as it bobbed their way, while Uncle Morten kept the *Anna Marie* a safe distance from the rock that had nearly finished the job the Russians had started earlier.

"It's getting closer," Peter reported back.

"Hey, Andersens!" came a shout from up ahead. "Is that you?"

"We're here!" Elise shouted back out of the wheelhouse door before Peter could say anything.

"Sorry to keep you waiting, Erik," yelled Uncle Morten. "We

were delayed with a minor mechanical problem."

"Glad you made it," replied Erik, this time close to the boat. Peter could barely make out someone else at the oars of a large, double-ended rowboat. From his perch in the closer end of the rowboat, Erik leaned out and flashed his light up at the deck of the *Anna Marie*. "We thought maybe you decided not to come back after all."

Almost, thought Peter as Uncle Morten eased their little fishing boat up behind the dory.

"Okay, follow us," said Erik. "There's a real low tide tonight, and we'll keep you away from the shallow spots. There's also a rock right behind us that you don't want to hit. . . ."

As if they were being towed into the little harbor, they idled in slowly behind the rowboat while Erik kept his light on for them to follow. They slipped past the jagged rock they had almost run into, and Peter and Elise returned to the warmth of the wheel-house.

At the wheel, Uncle Morten didn't take his eyes off the light ahead of them as they zigzagged through an invisible obstacle course. "This isn't the kind of harbor I'd like to try alone in the dark," he told them.

Erik and his friend knew just where they were going, though, and a few minutes later the rowboat glided quickly in past a dark row of fishing boats even smaller than the *Anna Marie*, then up to a small pier. Under a light from the shore, they finally caught a glimpse of Erik's cousin Evy, pulling up her oars.

"Right in there." Erik pointed with his flashlight to a space between two boats where they could tie up. Then he jumped out and trotted away, leaving Evy to tie up. She helped them wedge the *Anna Marie* securely in their spot between two sailboats.

"No one will see you here," she told them cheerfully. "At least for a few hours."

"Should we leave our bags on the boat?" asked Elise.

"We're not going to be here very long," answered Uncle Morten. "Just leave your coats on."

By that time, an old, familiar-looking car had returned to the pier and was flashing its lights.

"A taxi?" asked Uncle Morten.

"It's just Erik," explained Evy. "He's driving our friend's taxi-cab from church."

"Come on." Erik sounded the horn impatiently and leaned out the window. "I told Anders I would only be gone with his car for an hour this time. It's been two."

"Our fault," said Uncle Morten, slipping into the front seat. "Sorry we kept you waiting."

"That's okay." Erik looked in the rearview mirror to check on Peter, Elise, and Henrik. Elise gave him a big smile in the dark, which Peter saw, but Erik didn't notice. "I think we'll still make it in time for the sing-along. We were supposed to meet at the church at six-thirty."

"You think anyone will show up?" asked Uncle Morten as they pulled away from the pier. The old car jerked a couple of times, then stalled.

"Sure they'll show up." Erik sounded confident while he tried to get the engine started again. "People have been praying. They know what's going on."

"I wish *I* knew what was going on," said Henrik quietly.

Erik tried the starter once more. But just like before, the old car responded only with clicks and a groan. This time, the twins and Henrik knew the routine.

"We have to push start, Uncle Morten," announced Elise, opening the back door.

"What?"

Evy slipped out the other side. "It will just take a second if we all push."

With Uncle Morten's help, it was easier than before to get the ancient taxi started. A minute later, the engine popped and sputtered to life, and they all jumped back into their seats.

"Back to town," said Erik as they started down the winding road from Arnager to Ronne. Peter watched as Erik put the aging car through its gears.

"How do you do that?" Peter finally asked.

"Push in the pedal on the left there," explained Erik. "Then you move this handle, see?"

"I get it." Peter nodded, holding on as the car jerked. Everyone else was quiet until they drove into the city five minutes later.

Erik checked the road ahead. "I think there should be a few people at the church. After he heard what was going on, Pastor Lassen asked everyone to come."

"A few people?" asked Peter, leaning over the front seat to see. In the beam of their headlights, he made out dozens of people walking the same direction they were driving. And when Erik slowed down to park next to the Ronne church, there were at least a hundred people crowded around the front steps.

"Listen," said Elise, rolling down her window. "They're all singing."

Erik laughed. "That's why we're here. It's a Christmas sing-along. Only we're going to sing for the Russians."

Silent Night

"All right," said Erik, stopping the car next to the church. "Since you're supposed to be off the island, it's no good to let the Russians see you."

"But it's dark," began Henrik.

"It's dark, sure, but I found some scarves for you all to wear anyway. Put on the wool hats, too."

Peter found a dark blue wool cap and a scratchy scarf. "So what do we do, Uncle Morten? Are we going to sing, too?"

"Erik and I are going into the building up by the Castle to get Mrs. Melchior and Matthias," explained their uncle.

"And Evy is going to be driving," added Erik. "Right, Evy?"

"Right." Evy didn't sound as confident as her cousin, but she nodded several times.

"So I want you to stay in the car with her, out of the way," continued Uncle Morten. "We'll come back out of the building, try to blend in with the carolers, and then drive off as quickly as we can before the Russians discover what's happened."

By that time, the car was surrounded by carolers, all milling around and joining in the song. Peter even saw some kids who looked their age, along with parents and grandparents. Pastor Lassen stepped through the crowd and knocked on the car window on Evy's side.

"We're all going inside for a word of prayer," he told them as she rolled down her window. "You're just in time."

Peter could feel Henrik stiffen beside him while Elise opened her door and slipped out.

"Uh . . ." began Henrik.

"You want to wait here in the car?" asked Uncle Morten.

"No, I'll come," Henrik finally replied, following Elise. "I guess my grandpa wouldn't have minded."

Inside, the large church was completely dark except for two candles on the altar. It didn't seem much warmer inside than outside, but more and more people filled the aisles. Peter stopped counting at two hundred.

"I still don't get it," Henrik whispered to him. "Do all these people think they're coming to some kind of Christmas service? Do they know about us?"

Peter shook his head. "I don't know, Henrik, except what Evy told us."

Up in the front, Pastor Lassen raised his hands for everyone to quiet down. He was dressed just like everyone else, in a heavy winter overcoat, but he had removed his hat.

"I want to thank you all for coming to this unusual service." He cleared his throat. "Especially on such short notice. Evy and Erik have contacted probably every one of you to pray, and I know they appreciate the way you've responded. But I'm sure you'd like to see the people you've been praying for. Hans, is the door closed?"

A man in the rear of the church called back, "All clear."

"Good," continued the pastor. "Let's have the Andersens and their friend Henrik please come up so that we can all see them."

"Wait a minute," Peter heard Henrik whisper to himself under his breath. But Henrik was swept along as Evy and Erik escorted them down the center aisle toward the front of the church. They walked past a half-dozen ushers in the aisles, who were passing out handfuls of candles. By the time they reached the front, Peter's knees were shaking.

"The Bible tells us to take care of strangers," began Erik. "So I appreciate everyone coming out like this, especially on Christmas, to help Henrik get his mother back."

Peter didn't know what to do with his hands, so he stuffed them deep in his pockets and looked down at his shoes in the dim light from the candles. Erik kept talking.

"Evy explained to most of you that the Russians are holding Henrik's mother in the Castle—her and the pilot of the plane she arrived in. The Russians have no reason to keep them as prisoners on our island. So that's why we're all here."

The golden glow grew brighter as people in the aisles all lit their candles from their neighbor's light. Henrik noticed, too, and he watched the ceremony thoughtfully. Soon nearly everyone in the church held a lighted candle, a sight that sent shivers up Peter's spine.

"Remember what Matthias said about candles at your Hanukkah celebration?" Peter whispered into Henrik's ear.

Henrik nodded, and his eyes seemed misty. "My dad said it, too. 'Many candles can be kindled from one candle without making it less bright.'"

"So before we go out to sing for the Russians who are occupying our island," put in Pastor Lassen, "let's pray for them—and for us."

Peter couldn't remember what the pastor prayed. He couldn't even bow his head all the way. He couldn't take his eyes off the shimmering sea of candles, the sea of twinkling lights that had lit up in front of them. He peeked over at Henrik, who was rubbing his eyes.

"It's beautiful," whispered Elise. She was staring at the sight, too.

As they stood there, the pastor finished his prayer and dismissed the people before the sea of candles began emptying out of the church and into the night. Someone gave them each their own candle, and they were swept up in the singing, out into the cold, still night.

"Stay with Evy near the car," Uncle Morten shouted at them, wrapping a scarf around his face. "And stay away from any Russian soldiers, just in case they recognize you. We may have to leave again in a hurry."

Peter nodded. But as the crowd surged up the street toward the Castle, he couldn't even see Evy or the car; maybe she was following from behind. Up above, the starlit sky seemed to listen as their singing drifted through the quiet streets:

> Wisemen traveled by the star,
>   leading to our Lord so far;
> Now we have a light to guide us,
>   if we follow, He's beside us.
> We can come to Jesus Christ.
> We can come to Jesus Christ.

Peter tilted his head back to find the star they were singing about. It seemed so real, and a drop of hot wax rolled down onto his hand.

"Ow!" he cried, but he held on to his candle. Henrik chuckled.

"I got the hot wax treatment, too," he told Peter.

"I was just looking at the stars," said Peter. "We don't see as many back home."

"Doesn't seem like it," agreed Henrik.

"Come on, you guys," Elise told them. "I see Evy behind us."

Their teenage friend had finally pulled up in the taxi, driving slowly behind the crowd as it made its way through the harbor streets and up the hill to the Castle. Peter, Elise, and Henrik kept pace as they got closer to the place where they had seen Henrik's mother and Matthias getting out of the Russian car. Evy pulled over to the side of the road and turned off her lights.

"I'm parking here," she whispered as she climbed out of the car. "But let's get a little closer."

"What if they see us?" worried Peter, pulling his scarf higher, over his face.

"We'll stay back here in the crowd," she replied.

Before they reached the buildings, Peter noticed two men slip away from the crowd and disappear into the woods. He grabbed Elise's arm and whispered into her ear.

"There go Uncle Morten and Erik," he told her. "Watch where they go."

By that time, several Russians had come out of the building, smiling and clapping at the music. Peter sighed with relief when he didn't recognize any of them.

"More!" demanded one. "More sing!"

Pastor Lassen made his way to the head of the caroling crowd and raised his hands, then turned around to face the Russians.

"Your turn," he told them, pointing. "You sing."

For a minute, the Russians looked confused, but finally they understood and called something back into the building. Then four more soldiers appeared, one of them wearing a high-peaked officer's hat. The crowd was silent while the seven men cleared their throats and sang a low, rambling song in odd Russian tones. Everyone stood silently, their candles still burning, until the men finished with a swing of their arms.

"Let's give them a good one," cheered Pastor Lassen as the Russians stood standing on the front step of their office building, hands on their hips. Peter couldn't make out the expressions on their faces, but he was sure it had to be something like, "Let's see you top that!"

" 'High From the Christmas Green Treetop'!" yelled a man from the church crowd. *That will get their attention*, thought Peter, remembering the words of the lively Danish folk tune—a favorite for when families would hold hands and dance around their Christmas trees.

Pastor Lassen nodded his head at the suggestion and began singing the song. " 'High from the Christmas green treetop, the Christmas star is shining!' "

Everyone joined in with their loudest voices, singing verse after verse from memory. As the singing got louder and louder, more and more Russians came out to hear.

"Look at the side of the office," said Elise between verses. "They're trying to get in."

Peter lost track of the words when he saw two dark figures coming around from the back of the building and checking a side window. All the Russians had to do was look behind them to see what was going on. Peter shut his eyes tightly, and when he opened them a few seconds later, Uncle Morten and Erik were gone.

"Did they get in?" asked Peter.

"Shh," warned Elise. "We have to keep singing."

They did, making their way through all four verses of "Silent Night" twice, and another carol besides. And though they kept an eye out for the side window where Uncle Morten and Erik had slipped in, still they saw nothing.

"At least the Russians aren't getting tired of the singing yet," said Elise.

In the middle of the next Russian song, Henrik began to side-step to the edge of the crowd, pulling Peter along with him.

"What are you doing?" whispered Peter. "We need to wait here."

"Something's wrong," answered Henrik. "If they found Mother, they would have been in and out right away. I'm going to go get them."

Peter looked back at where Elise and Evy were standing. Neither had noticed yet that Peter and Henrik were gone. And Henrik was right. Something *was* wrong.

"Okay," agreed Peter, biting his lip. "Maybe . . ."

He didn't have time to finish his thought. Henrik slipped out the side of the crowd, rolling into the bushes, with Peter right behind him.

"Do you know where we're going?" whispered Peter. But by that time, they were already even with the building, and Peter could see lights through the branches of a berry bramble. One of the thorny bushes caught his jacket, tearing the sleeve.

"This way," whispered Henrik, crouching low. All they could see ahead of them was the side of the building and the same dark window where Uncle Morten and Erik had disappeared just a few minutes before.

"Are you sure we're doing the right thing?" asked Peter.

"Of course I'm sure," answered Henrik. Thankfully, the

woods came almost to the side of the building, giving them cover to within ten feet of the window. They would just have to run those few feet from the edge of the trees to the window. As long as none of the Russians were left inside. . . .

But maybe that's what happened to Uncle Morten, worried Peter.

Henrik sprinted away from behind a cluster of trees, but Peter wasn't far behind as they pressed themselves up against the side of the building. A quick glance to the front, and Peter could see half of the crowd. The Russians were still standing outside the front door, singing their lungs out.

"This is the window," whispered Henrik, lifting it with a tiny squeak. Peter slid in behind his friend, and they stood in a dark room. It had been easy. Too easy.

"Now where?" whispered Peter. He couldn't tell what kind of room they were in, only that there was a light coming from under the door. All they could hear was the singing. Peter didn't know what he would do if it stopped.

Henrik turned the doorknob silently, then slowly poked his head out. He motioned for Peter to follow, and Peter held his breath, following on tiptoe.

In single file, they padded silently down a stark hallway with several doors on either side. Peter took the right side, and Henrik the left, opening doors as they made their way down the hall. Each room was like the one they had come in from, however, and Peter's heart raced faster and faster as he thought of the Russian soldiers coming back into their office building. It must be getting cold for the men, standing outside the front door without their coats on.

Up ahead, the hallway opened into a larger room, maybe the front entry. Peter hesitated, and Henrik held up his hand. There, up ahead, two men were kneeling behind several large filing cabinets, their backs to the boys. Peter froze as Erik wheeled around silently and stared at them. Uncle Morten did the same.

Peter didn't know whether to run or stay where he was, but Erik frantically waved them off, as if a horsefly had attacked his face. Uncle Morten, looking almost as surprised, pointed up ahead at a door that just then swung open. Before Peter and Henrik could move, they were staring straight at a startled Lieutenant Riznik, the Russian translator.

UNEXPECTED ALLY

The surprise in the lieutenant's eyes lit up for only a minute before he held up his finger to stop Peter and Henrik from running. Peter wasn't at all sure he could run, anyway; his shoes felt nailed to the floor. Lieutenant Riznik looked toward the front door and motioned for them both to come.

"Us?" Henrik pointed at himself.

Lieutenant Riznik crossed his arms and frowned. "Quickly. I can help you."

"But—" protested Peter, looking from his uncle to the Russian. Uncle Morten stood up, looking as confused as Peter felt.

"Oh," said Lieutenant Riznik, not as surprised this time. "I should have known you would all show up here. Come with me quickly before the others come back inside. Is there anyone else?"

Erik stood up, but by that time the lieutenant had turned on his heel and opened the same door he had just come out of. Henrik was the first to enter a small, windowless room, with Peter close behind.

"Mother!" Peter heard Henrik exclaim, followed by the Russian's stern warning. Peter looked around the man to see Henrik hugging his mother, with a worried-looking Matthias Karlsson standing behind them, his hands on his head in surprise. His beard looked a little untrimmed, and there were dark lines under his eyes, but he smiled at Peter. When Mrs. Melchior finally let go of her son, Peter could see that she had the same tired look, along with a large bandage on her forehead.

"There's no time for that now," warned Lieutenant Riznik, pulling Henrik and his mother apart. "Just get out of here and don't come back. And if you are captured, I will deny ever seeing you. Do you understand?"

Uncle Morten caught the lieutenant by the shoulders as the man came back out of the room.

"Who are you, really? Do you work for the British, or something?"

The man chuckled. "Let's just say I'm not who you think I am."

Peter studied the man's face as he backed out of the room. "You telephoned us back home in Helsingor. I know you did."

Lieutenant Riznik impatiently waved them on. "You can believe that if you like. Now run the way you came in through the window. I'll try to keep them singing just a while longer. Go!"

This time Uncle Morten led the way down the hall, looking behind him once to see that everyone was following. Peter glanced back, too, and saw Riznik standing in the front room staring at them. He waved them on again. Peter hoped his eyes said "thank you" in a way the man could read.

The sound of laughter and singing grew louder as they heard the lieutenant opening the front door. The carolers hadn't yet run out of songs.

"Go!" repeated Uncle Morten, standing by the window to shepherd everyone through. First went Erik, then Matthias, then Mrs. Melchior and Henrik, and finally Peter.

"I sure wish you would have stayed back with the others, Peter," his uncle told him as they both huddled next to the building. Before Peter could say anything, his uncle gave him a push. "Now, Peter. Run!"

Peter sprinted away from the building, his mind racing.

Maybe Lieutenant Riznik would change his mind, he thought, or shout at them to stop. Or maybe one of the Russian soldiers standing by the front door of the building would happen to look back in their direction. A lot of the Russians had guns. . . .

Peter tried not to think of the danger. But only a few steps from the safety of the woods, something grabbed at his foot. A root, maybe. The next thing Peter knew, he had fallen on his face—hard.

Get up! he told himself. *Someone's going to see!*

Before he could move, Uncle Morten came up from behind and scooped him up like a puppet on a string. Peter felt himself lifted on his feet, and he practically flew to the shelter of the woods.

"Okay, let's keep down," whispered Uncle Morten when they were safely behind the trees. "But not quite *that* far down, Peter."

The others had to be up ahead, but Peter couldn't see through the thick bushes. He dusted himself off and stayed close to his uncle.

"I'm sorry, Uncle Morten," Peter finally whispered. He tried to step lightly as they slipped around toward where the carolers were standing. Uncle Morten said nothing but squeezed his arm gently as they got closer to the singing. Henrik and the others were crouching in the bushes just ahead, waiting.

"Okay," signaled Uncle Morten. "We're all here."

Almost as if they had rehearsed the entire operation, people from the church gathered around the group as soon as they stumbled back from the woods. Someone produced heavy coats for Mrs. Melchior and Matthias. Peter couldn't see what the Russians were doing at the front door of their headquarters, but it sounded as if everyone was saying good-night and Merry Christmas in Danish and Russian.

"Good thing we're not back at the restaurant," said Erik under his breath. "About this time, they'd be bringing out the vodka and expect us to have a toast."

As Peter found his way to the back of the crowd with the others, someone caught his sleeve.

"Where have you been?" asked Elise. "One minute you were here, and the next—"

She stopped short when she saw for the first time who was with them. Mrs. Melchior smiled shyly in the light of someone's candle stub. The dark blue coat she was wearing was too big for her, and the sleeves hung way past her hands.

"It's good to see you here, Elise," said Henrik's mother quietly. "You didn't all have to come, did you?"

Elise's mouth dropped open, but she snapped it shut and let go of Peter's arm. "Mrs. Melchior!" she croaked. "We, uh, we didn't know it would turn out like this."

"I can testify to that," agreed Uncle Morten, "or I would never have allowed them to come. You can help me tell that to their mother when we get home."

"Excuse me, folks," interrupted Erik. "But let me remind you that you're not home yet. We're still standing only a few hundred feet away from the Russian soldiers who were holding you prisoners just a few minutes ago. Let's get back to the car."

Matthias nodded seriously, turned, and almost knocked down a little boy who was standing next to him in the crowd. The boy, about five, stared up curiously. "Are you the man we've been praying for?" he asked matter-of-factly.

Matthias adjusted his round glasses and looked back at the others, then patted the little boy on the shoulder. "I suppose I am. And thank you very much."

"Come on!" Erik whispered anxiously as he held the back door to the taxi open. "We can talk later."

The crowd was moving back away from the Russian headquarters by that time, and as people discovered that Mrs. Melchior and Matthias were with them, they began to press around, shaking their hands and holding on to them.

"Look, we can't do this right now," objected Erik, looking across the crowd that was coming at them. "The Russians . . ."

Somehow they managed to slip out of the crowd and into the old taxi, with Erik, Evy, and Elise in the front, and Uncle Morten, Peter, Henrik, Mrs. Melchior, and Matthias in the wide rear bench seat.

"You're heavier than I thought," Henrik told Peter, who had to sit on his lap.

"Sorry." Peter held on to the seat in front of him for balance as Erik tried to start the car. Someone knocked on the window next to Henrik.

"Here's some more cookies, in case anyone is hungry," said a woman from outside, pushing in a plate of delicious-smelling Danish Christmas sugar cookies. They were Peter's favorite, the kind that looked like little flat donuts.

"Thank you, Mrs. Melgaard," said Evy from the front seat.

Henrik took the cookies and looked at Peter. "Do you understand why these people are being so nice to us?"

Peter popped a cookie into his mouth. "I think I know."

"Oh no," moaned Erik. He turned the key a few more times, but the car only clicked. "I should have guessed."

"Everyone out to push?" asked Evy.

"No, wait a minute," said Erik. He rolled down his window and leaned out. "Look out behind the car!" he called out as a warning. The crowd was still in front of the car, blocking their view of the Russians. Erik released the hand brake and let the taxi roll backward, tires crunching on gravel as they slowly gathered speed.

"Can you see out there?" asked Evy, sounding worried.

"No," replied Erik, "but I will in just a minute. Hold on."

A second later, the car jerked into gear and sputtered to life, still rolling backward. To the cheers of everyone in the car, he put on the brake and turned them around.

"All right," said Erik. "Now we'll get you out of here before someone discovers their two prisoners are missing."

Peter was afraid to say anything as they bumped down the familiar road to the airport. Finally Henrik cleared his throat.

"Are you okay, Mother?" he whispered. "Your head . . ."

"We're fine, Henrik. They didn't hurt us. I just bumped my forehead when we landed."

Matthias chuckled. "She's a trooper. Those Russians kept us up all night for two nights shouting at us. It's been exhausting."

Then his voice turned serious. "They were going to take us to Russia in the morning."

Henrik stiffened. "Why? All you ever did was land your plane here."

Matthias nodded. "The weather was not too good, so we came down for a break. All I can figure out is that we landed on their airstrip, and they thought I looked just like some spy they'd been looking for."

"I still can't believe that," added Henrik.

"A Swedish spy, if you can imagine," continued Matthias. "I'm just thankful you people came when you did. And I have to admit, it was great hearing those Christmas songs. But Peter and Elise, why are you here, too?"

Peter grinned in the dark car. "Henrik wouldn't let Uncle Morten go all alone, and we couldn't let Henrik go by himself."

"Well now, Peter," Uncle Morten corrected him. "You'd better explain that your parents only let you go because I told them it was just going to be a quiet trip to pick up these two."

"I appreciate that, Henrik," said Matthias. "I hope you don't hate me for getting your mother in all this trouble. And I hope you don't hate me for losing your dad's book with the letters."

Henrik didn't answer right away, but then he cleared his throat. "It's okay. We found it."

"You did?"

"In the plane. In Mother's purse. It's on the boat."

"Then you read the letter?"

"I did," whispered Henrik. "Did you?"

"Well, I thought I would help out by finding it for you. Seems like I've only caused more problems. I'm sorry."

Henrik sighed. "That's okay. Did you read the letter? About Jerusalem and all that?"

"Your mother read it to me. It was something your father and I had discussed before. . . ."

Peter tried listening to the others talking in the dark as they bumped along. Henrik asked more questions, and Matthias answered in a quiet, tired voice. They sounded almost like friends.

Peter thought about getting home . . . and about Tiger, lost some-where on Bornholm Island.

"Airport's coming up on the right," Erik finally announced.

"That's my stop," said Matthias, ending their conversation.

"Now wait a minute," objected Uncle Morten. "We're not—I mean, we had planned to take you all home on the boat."

"I appreciate that, Morten, but I'm not going to leave my plane here for the Russians to enjoy. I'm not used to giving Christmas presents, remember? I'm Jewish, after all."

Erik looked confused. "I was just going to drive you to the harbor, but whatever you folks want . . ."

"I'll go with you," volunteered Henrik. "As long as we're not going all the way to Jerusalem."

Matthias laughed at what had to be a private joke, and Peter remembered the mysterious letter from Henrik's father that had said something about Jerusalem. Peter looked curiously at his friend, the same one who had despised Matthias only a short time ago.

"All right," Uncle Morten finally agreed. "We'll help you get your plane."

Matthias opened his door. "I appreciate your offer, Morten, but . . ."

"Well, you can't do it alone, that's for sure," said Uncle Morten. "We'll help you get the plane out, and then Ruth and Henrik can ride back with us."

"We'll fly with Matthias," said Henrik once more. "That is, if it's okay. . . ."

Matthias paused, then turned around with a smile. "That's okay with me."

"Don't slam the doors," warned Erik. "I'm going to keep the car idling here with Evy. I don't want to stop it and not be able to start again. We'll probably need to get out of here in a hurry."

They were parked by the side of the road, about the same place they had parked when they came to the airport the night before. The main airport buildings were out of sight behind a small hill.

"Wait a minute," whispered Uncle Morten. "I think maybe the

kids should wait here in the car with you."

But Peter and Elise were already out and leading the way over the hill. Elise turned back and waved for her uncle to follow. "We know where everything is here, Uncle Morten. Come on!"

Uncle Morten grabbed a flashlight and followed, mumbling. "My brother is never going to forgive me when he finds out about this."

Henrik helped his mother and Matthias find their way over the path and the hill, then down toward the two airport buildings with the others. And just like before, only a faint light was shining from inside the airport office, next to the old German transport plane. The big hangar was as dark as ever.

"This way," whispered Peter.

"Any idea how many Russians are here?" whispered Uncle Morten.

"There were only three of them the other night," answered Henrik. "They're all probably just sitting around again playing cards."

As they tiptoed over to the hangar, Peter nodded at the high window he had crawled into before. "That's how we'll get in. It's easy to open."

While Henrik gave him a lift up to the window, Peter tried to jiggle it, just in case it was open.

"Why don't you try the door?" asked Elise, turning the doorknob on the door below the window. It swung open with a loud squeak.

Henrik let go of Peter's foot, leaving him to jump down. "Way to go, Elise!"

"Well, I would have tried that," explained Peter, "but—"

"That's okay," interrupted Uncle Morten, shepherding them all inside and shutting the door. They stood for a moment in the darkness before Morten snapped on Erik's flashlight and played its weak beam around the large hangar.

"It's over there," instructed Peter, guiding the flashlight beam with his hand. They all looked at the little red plane, sitting in the same spot it was before.

"So how are we going to get it out of here without the Russians stopping us?" Henrik asked the question Peter had been wondering ever since they stopped at the airport.

None of the adults answered for a moment, but as Matthias checked out his plane, Peter pulled Henrik aside.

"Hey, Henrik," he said to his friend. "See that rope over there?"

They could barely make out a coil of rope hanging on the wall next to a pile of other equipment and tools.

"I see it. What are you thinking?"

"I'm thinking that we need a way to slow down the Russians," answered Peter.

"What—should we go over and tie them up?" Henrik almost laughed.

"Kind of. All we really need to do is make it so they can't open the door right away. That should give you enough time to get away. Uncle Morten?"

Peter's uncle stepped up to where the boys were trying to reach the rope.

"I was thinking the same thing," Uncle Morten told them. "It's not going to stop them, but . . ." He reached over and hefted the large coil off the wall, then headed for the door.

"Where are you going, Morten?" asked Matthias from the plane. "We're almost ready."

"I'll be right back," answered Uncle Morten. "The boys and I are just going to take care of something for you."

Peter and Henrik crept back out into the night behind Uncle Morten.

"Not a sound," whispered Peter's uncle. "I'm going to attach the middle of the rope to the door, around the doorknob. You boys each take an end and wrap it around the building. Find somewhere to tie it off."

"Right," the boys answered in chorus.

"And stay away from the windows," warned Uncle Morten.

Peter held his breath as he watched the shadowy figure of his uncle tiptoe up to the door in the middle of the small airport building. It was more of a shed, really, with a tin roof and matching metal sides. He counted to ten before he took one end of the rope and Henrik took the other, and they approached the little building as if they were wrapping a Christmas present with a ribbon. Peter ducked down when he came to the lone window on his side, then continued crawling with the rope to the back of the building. Inside, he could hear the now-familiar sound of Russian soldiers laughing at what had to be their usual card game.

But there was no time to worry about the men inside. Peter met Henrik and Uncle Morten around the back of the shed.

"Good thing this little building isn't any bigger," whispered Henrik, holding up the end of his rope. Peter had just about the same length of rope left, too.

"Perfect," he agreed, tying a loop. Silently Uncle Morten joined the two ropes in one of his sailor's knots, then leaned back to tighten the "package" around the little building.

"That should hold them for a bit," he whispered. "Let's get back to the hangar."

Elise swung the door open for them when they returned. "Done?" she asked.

"Done." Peter tapped her shoulder as he slipped past her.

"I think we're ready here," announced Matthias from his airplane. "There's still plenty of gas in the tank, enough to get us back to Helsingor." Peter turned to Henrik as Matthias and Mrs. Melchior climbed inside the plane.

"Well, you're going to beat us home."

"Yeah," agreed Henrik. "It will take you a whole day by sea, but we'll be there in only a couple of hours. Maybe we'll come out and meet you."

Mrs. Melchior turned around from her seat in the little plane. "I wish we could thank those people again for all they did."

"We'll tell them," promised Elise. "We still have to get back to the *Anna Marie*."

Henrik was wedged into the tiny cargo area behind his mother.

"I still keep expecting that Erik guy to show up," Henrik told Peter through the airplane window as Peter helped his uncle and Matthias wheel the red plane closer to the hangar door. "He's going to step up in front of us and give us the bill for all this help. 'Here you go, Henrik,' he's going to say. 'Here's your bill for all our services, plus the services of the people in the church.' "

Peter laughed softly and shook his head. "You still don't get it, do you, Henrik?"

"And you do?"

"I think I figured it out when we were on Erik's grandpa's boat. Remember that Bible verse he made you read?"

"I remember the one about entertaining strangers and angels. Maybe I'll have to read that part again when we get home, if I can borrow your book again."

Peter smiled. "Sure thing."

Uncle Morten grunted as he pulled the front end of the plane around to face the right direction. "All right," he whispered. "Is everyone ready? Peter and Elise, you pull on those chains over there as fast as you can when I give you the signal. I'll be out in the middle of the runway with the flashlight so Matthias can see where to go. As soon as you get the door open, Peter, I want you two to run for the car. Got it?"

Peter and Elise both nodded.

"See you back home," said Uncle Morten. He carefully shut the door of the plane and gave it a pat for good measure. Then he slipped over to the entry door, peeked out to see that all was clear, and flashed the light at the twins.

"Pull!" said Elise, but Peter was already pulling as hard as he could. The heavy chain rattled and complained, and he was sure the Russians in the shed would hear them.

The dim flashlight bobbed over to what was probably the middle of the runway, then turned back and flashed in their direction. At the same time, the little airplane's starter whined, followed by a cough and then the throaty roar of the engine itself. Peter could feel a good set of blisters forming on his hands from the chain, but still he pulled until the giant metal garage door was almost up.

A hand came out from the airplane to wave, the engine revved up, and then the plane shot out of the hangar like a scared red rabbit. There would not be much time.

"See you at home!" Peter waved, but then Elise pulled him by the hand.

"Look, Peter," she cried. "We've got to run!"

A pair of headlights was bouncing over the rutted gravel drive leading to the airport from the highway, directly blocking the way back to the taxi.

"Yeah, but which way?" he answered as they took a couple of steps out of the building.

They stood frozen for a terrifying moment while a small jeep filled with soldiers and one very large, barking black dog raced up to the hangar. The only place for Peter and Elise to hide was behind a bare clump of bushes just outside the building. As they kneeled in the darkness, the jeep's tires shot gravel in their faces. If he had been quick enough, Peter could have grabbed the ankles of the soldiers piling out of their jeep. Three or four, maybe; he couldn't tell. Plus the dog. All he knew was that he would start a coughing fit from the exhaust if they didn't stand up or move away from their hiding place.

In all the shouting that followed, Peter wasn't sure if the soldiers were chasing Uncle Morten or the plane. By that time, it had taxied well out onto the runway where Uncle Morten was guiding them and was already picking up speed. Peter and Elise got to their feet slowly and peeked over the top of the jeep.

From the office shed where they had tied the doorknob shut, a window crashed, and one growling soldier tumbled outside into the dim light from a bare light bulb next to the door. He got to his feet, dusted himself off quickly, and gestured wildly at the door and at the plane.

The other soldiers were running back to see what had happened with the broken window while the soldier from the building was running toward the airstrip and pointing in the direction of Uncle Morten's light. A couple of other men were climbing out of the window, too.

What do we do? Peter's mind raced, then he looked down at the empty jeep.

"Hop in!" he whispered to Elise, jumping into the driver's seat.

"What?" Elise stared at him but didn't move. "Are you crazy? You can't drive."

"I saw how Erik did it. Come on, there's no time if we're going to save Uncle Morten. They're going to catch him with that dog!"

Elise reluctantly slipped into the passenger seat while Peter took a deep breath and felt for the gearshift, then the pedals. It would have to be just like Erik explained, or they would never make it. Peter was afraid to look to the side. The Russians would see what was going on any second.

"Okay, what did he say?" Peter asked himself. "The clutch is on the left. . . ."

"I don't know," replied Elise, hiding her face behind her hand. "But we better get going."

Peter didn't have time to experiment. He pushed down hard with his left foot, hoping he was pushing the right pedal. Then he took a knob in his right hand and tried to move it. *Which way?* Erik hadn't told him that part, so Peter decided he would push it forward as best he could.

Forward must mean go, he reasoned, jamming the gearshift into place. There was a kind of click, but nothing happened.

"Come on!" urged Elise. The Russians had switched on powerful flashlights and were starting to comb the airfield. The shadow of their large dog, growling and choking on a leash, was leading the way.

"Okay, okay, but I can't remember. Push down, in gear, put on the gas. . . . There are too many things to do all at once."

For a second, Peter thought to himself that he had made a big mistake. But he squeezed his eyes shut, raced the engine with his foot on the gas pedal, and let go with his left foot.

The jeep seemed to lift off the ground with all four wheels, screeching out of the gravel and jerking like a wild horse set free.

"Peter!" yelled Elise, clutching the seat so she wouldn't fly out.

When Peter opened his eyes, they were flying down the runway and he was holding on to the steering wheel for dear life, his knuckles white. The engine was screaming, but Peter didn't dare try to shift gears the way Erik had done with the taxi. They were moving, and that was all that counted to Peter.

But they were also going to run down the Russian soldiers and the dog, or at least it looked that way when they caught the soldiers with their headlights. The jeep jerked crazily on as Peter swerved to the right. The soldiers dove to the left.

"Uncle Moor-ten!" Peter screamed at the top of his lungs. Elise was still hanging on in the passenger seat. "Uncle Moor-ten!"

Peter knew that the plane had to be gone by that time, but Uncle Morten was still out in the darkness somewhere. *Why doesn't he just flash his light at us?* Peter wondered. Then Elise took up the yell.

"Uncle Morten!" she shouted, standing up at her seat. Peter swung around in the middle of the airstrip. From somewhere behind them, they could hear the Russians' police dog yelping. As the sound grew louder, Peter realized they had let the animal go.

"Uncle Morten!" Peter yelled once more, and then his uncle was standing directly in front of them, caught like the Russians had been just seconds ago in the jeep's headlights.

Suddenly it occurred to Peter that he wasn't sure how to stop. He knew there was one more pedal on the floor somewhere, but which one? He started stomping on the floor until he found it. Uncle Morten sidestepped them as they skidded by, but Peter stepped even harder on the pedal he had found, and the jeep screeched and jerked to a stop. The engine died at the same time.

Peter somersaulted into the little backseat as Uncle Morten vaulted into his place behind the wheel. The Russians' flashlights were coming into view. Without a word, their uncle expertly started the car and pulled away. Peter glanced back once more to see a dark shape shoot out of the darkness, snarling and snapping.

"Their dog, Uncle Morten!" Peter warned him just as the animal lunged at Peter's arm on the back of the jeep. Peter yanked his hand back, but the dog closed his teeth on the sleeve of his jacket, nearly pulling him out onto the runway. Elise gripped

Peter by the collar in a desperate tug-of-war as Uncle Morten steered them off the paved part of the airstrip.

With a loud rip, Peter's sleeve gave way, and the determined dog tumbled behind them with only a mouthful of fabric.

"Nice doggy," gasped Peter, falling back on his seat. "Thanks, Elise."

They jolted through a gully and bumped up a hillside, slid around a couple of bare trees on the crest, and nosed back down to the highway. Only a few hundred feet down the road, Erik and Evy were waiting in the same place they had left them. Uncle Morten pulled up behind the old taxi, and they jerked to a stop. "Everyone into the taxi," ordered Uncle Morten. "We don't want to be driving this thing around."

Peter was glad to hop out of the jeep, and he shuddered at the thought of what he had done. *I'm not going to get behind the wheel of another car for a long, long time*, he promised himself, hurrying toward the waiting taxi. Evy pushed the doors open from the inside.

"Wait a minute," said Uncle Morten, running back to the jeep. "There's one more thing I have to do, just in case anyone was thinking of following us." He reached across the steering wheel, grabbed the keys out of the ignition, and tossed them into the bushes next to the road.

"So where did that jeep come from?" asked Erik, once they were safely away from the airport.

"That's what I'd like to know," said Uncle Morten.

"Well," Peter cleared his throat. He looked at his uncle in the light from the rearview mirror, hoping for a clue that would tell him if he was in trouble or not. But the light grew brighter, and Peter squinted. Erik groaned from the driver's seat.

"I think someone's following us," he announced.

FOLLOW THE STAR

"The Russians again?" asked Elise. She and Peter turned around to look out the taxi's little oval back window.

"Maybe. I'm not sure," admitted Erik, speeding up a little more. The headlights stayed with them but made no attempt to catch them or pass. "All I can tell is that there's more than one car. Three or four in a row."

"Are you sure they're following us?" Elise sounded nervous.

Erik sighed. "After tonight, I don't know. But we're almost to the harbor. See if they turn off the main highway with us."

The growing parade of headlights behind them turned off at the side road to the harbor, then pulled up to the pier where they had left the *Anna Marie* just a few hours earlier.

"What are all these cars?" wondered Evy, looking around at the crowd. Before they could step out of the car, a man was knocking on the driver's window.

"Grandpa Torp!" exclaimed Erik, rolling down his window.

"We've been waiting for you," said Erik's grandfather, looking around at the dozen or so cars that had parked there. Several more were pulling up to the pier as they spoke.

"Seems the Russians figured out that their 'spies' have disappeared," continued Grandfather Torp, "and now we hear they're checking all the ports to make sure no one gets away by sea. They have their own patrol boat out there to make sure." He waved his hand at the ocean for emphasis.

"Are they here?" asked Uncle Morten, stepping around from his side of the car.

The old man shook his head. "Not yet. But we have your boat warmed up and ready to go. We even pumped out a little water. I wouldn't wait if I were you."

"But won't they catch up with us?" worried Elise.

Grandfather Torp put his hand on her shoulder. "You don't need to worry about a thing, angel. Just get in your uncle's boat and have a good trip home. Come back and visit us again, too."

The old man looked straight at Peter. "And there's a present for you in your boat, Peter. A box."

Peter nodded but wondered. "Is it—I mean, what?"

The old man chuckled. "It's not from me. It's from that big guard who was watching you down on the pier. He came with it just after you left, and he kept saying, 'for boy, for boy.' I don't know how he knew."

"Knew what?" asked Peter. But Uffe Torp just smiled.

Evy gave the twins both a hug, then disappeared while Erik shook their hands.

"Thanks for everything," said Peter.

"I think your friend didn't quite understand what was going on with all these crazy Christians coming out to help," said Erik. "Did you?"

Peter nodded and smiled as he stepped down to the deck of the *Anna Marie*. "We did some reading about it. I'll explain it to him when we get home. I promise."

"All right, then. Be sure you do." Erik saluted them from the shore, and Peter finally noticed what was going on around them.

Engines were starting up around the cozy little harbor, and red and green night running lights winked on in dozens of fishing boats. Then, one by one, candles began appearing in the back windows of each boat.

"It's like the sing-along all over again," said Elise, standing out on the deck.

"Follow us out of the harbor," yelled someone from the boat ahead. Uncle Morten flashed his lights in response. Erik, Evy, and their grandfather waved from the pier just above their heads.

"Hey, don't forget this," yelled Erik. He held up a candle, then tossed it at Peter. "Catch!"

Peter picked up the candle off the deck, then held it up.

"Thanks!" he called back. "Thanks for everything!"

Uncle Morten followed the parade of lighted boats out of the harbor, and Elise lit their candle and placed it in the window just like everyone else. When he stepped out on deck for a minute, Peter heard a family singing up ahead, the sound of their voices drifting across the still waters.

" 'Silent Night,' " he whispered back to Elise. "They're singing 'Silent Night.' "

"I hear it," agreed Elise. "But what's that other funny sound?"

Peter listened carefully, and this time it was clear, even above the sound of the engine. A cat was meowing sadly somewhere nearby.

Elise looked out at the lights. "Must be on the shore some-where."

"No, it's not." Peter turned his head like radar to home in on the sound, then followed it back into the wheelhouse.

"Do you hear that cat, Uncle Morten?" asked Peter. Just then they both heard a loud wail.

"There, hear it?" asked Peter.

Uncle Morten looked around the wheelhouse while Peter grabbed a flashlight to discover a large cardboard box on the bunk behind them. The Christmas present from Uffe Torp!

"It's coming from this box, Uncle Morten!" Peter tore away the flaps of the box and looked inside to discover a frightened cat looking up at him. Its nose was badly scratched, and fur was missing in several large spots around its head. But there was no mistaking the striped pattern on its face.

"Tiger!" yelled Peter, gathering the animal up in his arms. "You made it after all!"

"Well, what on earth?" sputtered Uncle Morten.

"Erik and Evy's grandpa said the big Russian brought him something. That guy must have found Tiger after I tried to tell them I was looking for my cat!"

Tiger had settled into Peter's arms with a loud purring, but Peter held him up for a better look. Elise came in to see for herself.

"Look who's back," announced Uncle Morten.

"Wow, he looks like he's been pretty beat up," said Elise.

Tiger continued to purr, and Peter set him gently down on the bunk. "Pretty scratched up, but he's tough."

As a gentle swell began to rock them, Peter could see the other boats spreading out in different directions, a sea of candles below a sea of stars above. Then from around the dark outline that Peter recognized as the south coast of the island, another dark shape appeared.

"I'll bet that's the Russians," reported Uncle Morten. "Only this time, they don't want us to go. Better put your cat back in his box."

"What about the candle?" asked Peter.

Uncle Morten nodded. "Blow it out. From here on we have to follow the stars."

Elise blew out their candle, and they all looked up through the front windshield. Twinkling above them, they could see the bright highway of glitter called the Milky Way. Peter's father had taught him how to find the Big Dipper, then Polaris, the North Star. That would be the way home, and the bright star twinkled like a signpost. Everything else on the *Anna Marie* was dark, and Uncle Morten pushed the engine to full throttle.

Behind them, dozens, maybe hundreds, of candles still glowed brightly, and the Russian patrol boat was stopping at each light.

"They're still checking for spies," mumbled Peter. Even though the Russians could easily outrun them and were heading their direction, Peter didn't feel scared for the first time all evening. He looked in the direction of the North Star once more and tried to fight the heaviness in his eyelids that suddenly made him want to curl up in the corner and go to sleep.

"We'll be home by morning," Uncle Morten assured him. Peter felt a big hand on his shoulder. He leaned back into the bunk behind the steering wheel and let his eyes close. Tiger had crawled out of the box and curled up beside Peter. Between the steady chugging of the *Anna Marie*'s engine and the cat's contented purring, he fell asleep dreaming of carolers singing "Silent Night."

———————

When Peter woke, he could still hear singing, but this time it was the low bass voice of Uncle Morten, singing one of the same Christmas tunes the people back on the island had sung. The one with the part that went, "Now we have a light to guide us; if we follow, He's beside us." Only Uncle Morten didn't quite know all the words, and there were a few "la-las" to fill in the blanks. Peter tried to rub the sleep out of his eyes.

"Oh boy, I must have dozed off for a little while," said Peter, slipping out of the bunk and straightening his neck.

"Try ten hours," replied his uncle. "You and Elise both have been out cold all night."

"No, really?" Peter looked outside. To the east, an apricot-colored sunrise told him his uncle was right. Tiger was keeping watch from a perch in front of the steering wheel. "Where are we?"

Uncle Morten pointed into the morning sky ahead of them. "Helsingor is coming up right there."

Behind them Elise yawned, stretched, and emerged from her corner of the bunk like a bear coming out of hibernation.

"Good morning, young lady," said Uncle Morten. "Now that you kids have warmed up a spot for me, I'm going to go back and catch a wink before we get home. Someone left some food for us in that box over there before we left. Peter, would you please keep us on this course? Don't let the cat eat all your break-fast. You'll see Kronborg Castle in a half hour."

"Sure." Peter stepped up to the wheel as Elise found them a morning snack of cheese, hard rye bread, and dried, smoked fish jerky. The way his stomach was rumbling, anything tasted good. Tiger liked the jerky, batting at it as if it were a toy.

"Who left us the food, Uncle Morten?" asked Peter, unwrap-ping a piece of cheese.

But their uncle was already snoring just behind them. Up ahead, Peter strained to make out the familiar outline of the shore around their home as they began to emerge from the dawn. He started to hum the same song his uncle had been singing.

"Henrik never did understand why all the people on the is-land helped us, did he?" asked Elise quietly.

"He will. I'm going to tell him."

Up above, most of the stars were gone, except a single bright one still hovering just above the dark blue-black horizon. And in the distance, Peter thought he could make out the towers of Hel-singor's Kronborg Castle.

"What star is that?" Peter asked his sister, even as the light seemed to get closer and brighter.

Elise looked out the window, then found some matches and lit the candle they had been given before to put in their window. "It's not a star, Peter. Look who's coming out to meet us."

His sister was right. The star they had been watching was really the bright light from a small airplane approaching them from the direction of home. A minute later, the pilot caught sight of them, and a little red plane circled around above the *Anna Marie* several times. Peter and Elise couldn't quite see who was inside, but they both knew.

Peter pushed open the wheelhouse door to stand out on the forward deck and waved a hand over his head. Outside the cold, salty breeze ruffled his hair like a flag, but it felt good.

"We're home, Henrik," he yelled up to the plane. "We're all home."

EPILOGUE

For most of Denmark, World War II ended on May 5, 1945, when German forces surrendered. One place they did not surrender right away, however, was on the little Danish island of Bornholm, far out in the Baltic Sea. Here the war would not end with a party, but with a terrible bombing. That's the true-life setting for this story.

Impatient with the Germans who would not surrender to them, Soviet (Russian) airplanes bombed Bornholm's two largest cities, Ronne and Nexo. The Russians caused heavy damage with their bombs, but the Germans did finally leave.

Then, as soon as the Germans left, the Soviets surprised everyone by sending eight thousand soldiers to set up camp on the island. They built their own barracks and even put up their own road signs.

But no one had asked the Danes for permission. Bornholmers weren't at all happy about having so many uninvited "guests." Still, they got along as best they could, and many of the Russians tried to be friendly. After all, the war was officially over, and the Soviets had fought against the Germans, too.

It was an odd chapter in Danish history, one they called "The Russian Time." The people of Bornholm wanted the Soviets to go home. Mostly, they were tired of having soldiers on the island. There were misunderstandings and some fights. And many of the people of Bornholm felt forgotten and a little abandoned.

No one is quite sure of the actual Russian plan for Bornholm, or why they stayed so long after the end of the war. It's possible they wanted to include this strategic island in the larger Soviet Union as a special military base. If so, that plan was never carried out. The Russians left for home eleven months after they arrived, and the last Russian troops left Ronne Harbor by April 5, 1946— to the great relief of the people of Bornholm, Denmark.

From the Author

One of the best parts of writing is hearing back from the people who read THE YOUNG UNDERGROUND stories. If you have any questions about these books, or just want to drop me a line, please feel free to write care of Bethany House Publishers, 11300 Hampshire Avenue South, Minneapolis, Minnesota 55438.

Robert Elmer